RAINE ENGLISH

DATE WITH A *VAMPIRE*

Elusive Dreams Press

DATE WITH A VAMPIRE

Published by Elusive Dreams Press

Copyright © 2013 Raine English

Excerpt from *Tin Angel* by Raine English copyright © by Raine English

Print ISBN: 978-1-62935-005-9

Digital ISBN: 978-1-62935-006-6

Edited by Linda Ingmanson

Cover by Char Adlesperger

www.RaineEnglish.com

First electronic publication: September 2013

First print publication: October 2013

The Tempted Series

Book One: DATE WITH A VAMPIRE

DEDICATION

To my daughter, Nikki, whose love of vampires nearly equals my own.

ACKNOWLEDGMENTS

Thank you to Linda Ingmanson for her editing, input, and friendship.

PROLOGUE

Dragesa Castle, Moldavia, 1523

The soldiers' death chants penetrated the tower's thick stone walls. It wouldn't be long before they reached Dragesa. Ambrus LeBreque scribbled the last of his notes, then slammed the ledger shut. He handed it, along with an amber-colored vial, to Blakesley, his long-time confidant.

Blakesley tucked the ledger under his arm, the folds of his black cape concealing it from view. "Sir, it may not be too late to escape."

Ambrus shook his head. "And have Berta and Cato burned at the stake in my place? No, I'll gladly give my life to save my wife and son. Besides, this damn potion is killing me anyway."

"That may not be so, sir." Blakesley rolled the vial between his fingers while he studied the potion inside. "It did make you appear human, at least for a time."

Ambrus doubled over in pain, letting out a loud groan. "Now it's burning a hole through my stomach." His confidant took a step forward, but Ambrus held his hand out to stop him. "There's nothing you can do to help. I'll be dead before dawn, and it's just as well, as

1

I'm to blame for this damned curse."

"Sir, you mustn't say that. It's not true. You didn't deserve to have your kingdom darkened."

"Perhaps not, but I did steal Berta from Lazlo, causing him to cast the spell that turned us all into vampires." He walked over to the window. An orange glow cut through the night. Torches. Lazlo's soldiers had arrived. He turned to Blakesley. "Find a place to hide my notes and the potion."

Lazlo was a powerful sorcerer, but Ambrus was a wizard too, and he'd worked years on a potion that would reverse the curse. Unfortunately, Lazlo heard of his experiments and given him a choice: his life in exchange for his wife's and son's safety.

"Sir, there must be something that can be done."

"It's too late, my friend." Sweat broke out along his brow and a chill ran down his spine at the thought of the fate that awaited him. A second later, the door burst open and Berta ran into his arms. Tears streamed down her lovely oval face. "Shhh," he whispered against her cheek. "You mustn't cry, my love."

She hugged him to her. "I can't let you do this—give up your life. It's my fault that Lazlo, the beast, is hell-bent on revenge. If I go to him… Beg him… Maybe he'll—"

Ambrus cut off her words sharply. "Do what? Kill you instead. No, my love, I'm afraid this is my fate alone." She tugged at his shirt, trying to pull him toward the door, but he held his stance. "I need you to be brave for Cato. Can you do that for me?"

She didn't answer.

Her legs wobbled, and he caught her around the waist before she hit the floor. "Berta, I shall always be with you and Cato…in your hearts." He pressed his mouth to her soft lips and kissed her one last time.

Outside, the chanting grew louder. She needed to leave Dragesa now. He did not want her viewing his execution. He scanned the room for Blakesley and found him standing in the doorway with a trembling Cato by his side. "Son, come here."

Cato stepped forward. Fear creased his young face, and Ambrus squeezed his shoulder. "You are a boy, yet soon you'll rule Dragesa. Be a just leader, my son, as I have tried to be. Do not let your dark desires guide you, for it would be easy to do, as our need for blood make us thieves in the night." He removed a leather cord from around his neck and placed it around Cato's. The gold lion-head pendant glowed richly. The necklace had been passed down to each LeBreque heir.

Cato stroked the pendant with his forefinger. His eyes misted over. "Father, I will make you p-proud."

"I have no doubt." He hugged his wife and child, then motioned for Blakesley. It was time for Berta and Cato to go. A coach waited in the rear courtyard to take them to town. They would stay with friends until Blakesley deemed it safe for them to return.

After they left, Ambrus took a deep breath and summoned all the courage he possessed before heading downstairs. He could do this. He must. For his family's sake.

Lazlo stood on the cobblestone walkway, his chest puffed out with smug satisfaction. Behind him, a sea of soldiers awaited his command. Ambrus was not about to let them sense his fear. He straightened his shoulders, pushed out his chin, and held his head high. He walked proudly, looking straight into Lazlo's steely eyes. "Remember your promise. No harm shall come to my family."

A wry smile twisted Lazlo's thin mouth. "Don't worry, having you gone and your kingdom cursed to an eternity of darkness is revenge enough."

Ambrus took one last look at Dragesa. The old stone castle was an imposing structure. Built to withstand time, it would house generations of LeBreque rulers for centuries to come. The thought brought him peace. He was ready for his death.

CHAPTER ONE

Present Day

Melody Johnson's heart pounded. Her fingers trembled. She stared at the lottery ticket clenched in her hand, then glanced over the rim of her reading glasses to check for the umpteenth time the numbers shown on the television screen.

Yup. They all matched. She swallowed hard. Holy cow! She was a multimillionaire. Rich beyond her wildest dreams. One-hundred-million-dollars rich. If she held the only winning lottery ticket, that was. But she wasn't greedy. Even if there were other winners, she'd be happy with whatever her share came to. She was about to have a lot more money than she'd ever dreamed of having.

She could even quit her job. Think of that—never having to shelve another book again. Although she loved working at the Reader's Den, the tiny bookstore paid only slightly more than minimum wage, and it could be years till a position opened at the library. Mrs. Smith had commanded the front desk for as long as Melody could remember yet showed no signs of retiring anytime soon. Melody had always wanted to be a librarian, but she didn't want to leave her small hometown of Hope, New York, to do so. She'd grown up there. Her friends and family all lived there. And it was only an hour outside of New York City. Everything she could ever want was in Hope.

Besides, money had never mattered much. She shared the two-story townhouse apartment with her three best friends. They paid their bills on time and had a few bucks left each month for a night on the town—usually spent at Chucky's Bar and Grill sucking down margaritas and splitting an order of nachos supreme. What more could a girl want? She'd always figured she had plenty of time to worry about her financial future. Yet, it looked like that had all been taken care of for her, and it had only taken a trip to the convenience store for a box of dog biscuits for her little black pug, Gizmo.

She never bought lottery tickets, mainly because she just never thought to. Today had been different, though. When the clerk handed her the two dollars in change, it was as if someone stood beside her and whispered lottery numbers in her ear.

Melody stared at the paper in her hand. If this was an indication of the power of intuition, she'd make sure to listen to all her inner urgings from now on. Sliding the sleeping pug off her lap, Melody hoped her legs were now steady enough to support her. She rose from the couch and bolted upstairs to wake her childhood friends. Mags, short for Margaret, shared a room with Billy, aka Willamina, while she bunked with Ann, not short for anything.

As she ran down the hall, her gaze drifted to the lottery ticket in her hand. Just a few minutes ago she'd been your average twenty-four-year-old, and now… Well, her life would never be the same. What lay ahead, she couldn't even begin to imagine.

⎄⎅

Blood trickled from the corner of Guystof LeBreque's mouth. He grimaced and wiped at it with the back of his hand. The taste of his kill lingered on his tongue. He couldn't wait to get home to rinse his mouth. For nearly four hundred years, he'd scoured the earth, hunting unknowing victims to quell his hunger and hating himself for it. Why couldn't he have been more like his younger brother, Theo, who loved everything about being a vampire?

Guystof raced through the fog-filled streets of London, darting in and out of shadowy alleyways toward his flat on the outskirts of the city. The memory of the dead man with two perfect holes piercing his neck, his drained body abandoned to the shadows, turned his stomach. Why had Guystof been condemned to live this eternal nightmare? His only salvation lay in his choice of victims: criminals of the worst degree.

He skirted the piles of garbage lining the streets. A horrible stench permeated the air, adding to his nausea. The sun had begun to crest the horizon, and he shielded his eyes with his hand. If he didn't hurry, he'd burn. Only once in his life had he experienced the dreadful bubbling—nearly two hundred years ago—yet the memory was as fresh as if it had happened yesterday. The pain had been almost intolerable, for not only his skin was affected. He'd begun to boil internally too, and if Theo hadn't dragged him inside, he would have been reduced to nothing more than a melted puddle of flesh. The sun was his enemy, more powerful than any vampire-hunting assassin.

Guystof dashed over the cobblestone street, his black cape billowing behind him like the wings of a bat. He spotted his flat up ahead and heaved a sigh of relief. His muscles ached with exhaustion. He longed for sleep. When he slid his key in the lock, his fingers started to tingle. He'd made it home just in time.

Inside the safety of his flat, he leaned against the thick wood door. Beads of sweat lined his brow, and a drop rolled onto his cheek.

"Still living on the edge, I see."

Guystof froze. What was his brother doing here? There was no mistaking Theo's thick Romanian accent. He never tried to conceal it, thinking it added to his charm. Guystof scanned the darkened room for him. The squeak of the rocking chair and the glow of a cigarette gave away his location.

Guystof left the foyer and crossed into the parlor, pointing his finger at the stone hearth. A fire exploded, and flames shot through the iron grating. The sudden light waved across the old Victorian parlor, touched on the dark oak furniture and Aubusson carpeting. He rarely used his powers, and almost never to do something he could just as easily do manually, but he needed to see his brother's face to decipher the real reason he'd come to call. Guystof knew him well enough to know his words alone might not provide the truth. Though he cared deeply for Theo, and owed him his life, he was not fool enough to trust him completely, for there was a side to him that no one knew. He'd betray his family if it served his purpose.

"A little longer out in the light and I fear I'd be treating you again, brother. Stirs up memories, doesn't it? Only this time might have proved more difficult. We're not in our country. These Brits don't look so kindly on our type."

Guystof studied Theo, outlined by the flickering orange flames. Although it had been more than a century since he'd seen him, his brother looked unchanged—shorter and stockier than he, with a face and body women adored. His blond curls were the complete opposite to Guystof's straight dark locks. Theo's boyish good looks were a tool he used to his advantage, but beneath his handsome facade lay a heart as dark as the devil's own.

Guystof leaned against the mantel, crossing one polished black shoe in front of the other. "What brings you to these parts? I know you haven't come merely to save my neck."

"That hurts. Why assume I don't care about your well-being?" The faintest hint of a smile graced his full lips, making him look oddly effeminate.

Guystof narrowed his eyes. Theo was toying with him and enjoying it. "You're fully aware no offense was meant, so let's cut to the chase, shall we?"

"All right, old boy, we'll save the small talk for later. You were right. I haven't come of my own accord. Father sent me." Theo leaned forward in the chair and reached into his back pocket, drawing out a crumpled piece of parchment. "I'm to give you this." He handed over the paper with a look Guystof couldn't decipher.

After unfolding the letter, he began to read. His brow furrowed and he waved the paper out in front of him. "How long have you had this?"

Theo took a drag on his cigarette and exhaled a long line of smoke. "You're not an easy man to find. I traveled Europe for weeks before finding your quaint little London abode."

"Nonsense. Tessa knows my whereabouts," Guystof said harshly, aggravated by this game.

"You don't know?" Theo's eyes glistened. Were those tears?

His fingers tensed on the paper. Something had happened. "Know what?" His voice cracked when he spoke.

"Tessa's gone. Killed by an assassin."

Guystof squeezed his eyes shut and clenched his jaw. It had happened again... Memories of another time and place whirled through his mind. His own mother had been killed by assassins, when he was only sixteen. Her death had been so painful that he'd never forgotten the agony on her face. After that tragedy, he'd vowed to never turn a woman into a vampire. He'd travel through eternity alone rather than risk losing someone he loved that way again. Yet it had happened...this time to his beloved Tessa... And she'd always been so careful too. That didn't seem to matter, though. A woman turned as an adult never acquired the skills necessary to protect herself from her enemies. It had only been a matter of time before she faced an excruciating death.

He crossed the room and stood beside Theo, placing his hand on his brother's shoulder. "I'm so sorry. I loved her too." Although she hadn't been his natural mother, he'd cared for her as such, and she'd returned his love by treating him as her own. She'd never showed Theo preferential treatment. Both boys had been raised under her careful tutelage.

"Is that the reason for this?" Guystof's gaze filtered down to the letter he held limply in his hand.

Theo shook his head. "Father's devastated. He'll not marry again. He's barely able to hunt for food, let alone raise enough money to keep Dragesa afloat. The castle needs repairs, to say nothing of the state of ruin the grounds have fallen into."

"But I can't marry. I took a vow."

Sneering scorn crossed Theo's handsome face. "That was no vow. Merely a silly promise you made to yourself as a boy. Now it's up to you to carry on the family legacy. You must choose a bride, and select wisely. You'll need one with a fortune," he said with a snicker. "Oh, and remember, you've only sixty days."

Guystof reread the letter, more carefully this time. When he finished, he directed his gaze back to Theo. "Father says nothing about the reason for the rush."

"Why prolong the inevitable? We all know you won't come through."

"And if I don't?"

Theo's eyes glittered dangerously, and a smug smile curved his mouth. "Then you'll no longer be a LeBreque. Father will disown you, and I shall become the family heir. We've ruled for centuries, and I'm not about to let the LeBreques lose that honor. Besides, I'll have no problem finding a mate. Of that, you can be sure."

The impact of Theo's words was not lost on Guystof. If he failed, not only did he face disgrace, but the kingdom would become a much more dangerous place. Theo loved nothing better than the taste of blood, and with him in control, there'd be nothing to stop him and his twisted desires.

Ⅎ⁥⁍

"Don't answer it," Melody shouted from the living room, wishing the phone would stop ringing. Her roommates chattered in the kitchen, preparing dinner. Just a week had passed since she'd gone to lottery headquarters and learned she held the only winning ticket, making her New York's latest most-eligible female, yet the word had spread like wildfire. It seemed everyone wanted a piece of her.

"I want my old life back," she said wistfully while sinking onto the couch. She scooped up the pile of messages the girls had taken for her and fanned through them.

"Sorry, Mel, that'll never happen." Ann entered the room, carrying a tray filled with chips and dip. She set it down on the coffee table in front of Melody, then snatched the papers from her hands. "I'm afraid these are just the beginning. Not only are you rich, but you're single. And being gorgeous doesn't hurt, either. You're one hot commodity, babe."

Melody groaned. "I don't want to be a hot commodity. I just want to be me, unknown old Melody from Hope."

Ann dropped the messages on the table, took hold of Melody's hand and pulled her to her feet. She dragged her over to the wall mirror. "Look, Mel, with a face and figure like yours, there's no way the media's going to keep you from the spotlight."

Big blue eyes stared back at her as she studied her reflection. A nice straight nose and full lips rounded out her heart-shaped face, while long strands of honey-colored hair draped her shoulders.

"Face it. You're America's new sweetheart."

Melody rolled her eyes.

"Get used to it. This is only the beginning."

"How am I going to live my life? How are we going to live? The phone never stops ringing." Her gaze scanned over the roses, carnations, and various other flowers spilling out from the vases sent to her by an endless stream of gold-digging men. "Seems like everyone in town now knows where I live." She turned to face her friend. "It's not fair to you…to any of you guys…but where can I go and not be found? What can I do to change all this?"

She crossed the room and plopped back onto the couch. Picking up a handful of messages from the table, she began to read. "'I'm a single white male, thirty-five, who would love to love you.'" She made a face and tossed the paper onto the floor. "Here's another one. 'Although I'm fifty-seven, don't let my age scare you. I can teach you things that young guys don't even know exist.' Yuck." She crumpled the message and threw it on the floor along with the other one. "And the list of Hope's single men goes on and on," she said, fanning the rest of the letters.

Ann's eyes grew wide and her jaw dropped open. "I've got it, I've got it," she shrieked, jumping up and down.

Melody scowled. "Oh, not you too. Don't tell me there's someone you want to fix me up with."

"Not someone. Twenty someones."

"What?"

Ann spread the papers over the coffee table. "Oh, where is it? I only just took the message this morning."

Melody patted her friend's arm. "Calm down. Where's what?"

"The message from the producers of *Dream Girl.*"

Melody groaned, and her fingers tightened around Ann's upper arm. "You're not going to tell me what I think you are, are you?"

Ann's eyes sparkled with excitement. "Well, if you think they want you to be the next Dream Girl, then yes, that's what I'm telling you."

She took a deep breath and coaxed Ann onto the couch. "Sit here and listen very carefully. I am not going to be the next anything. I don't want any TV appearances or interviews of any kind. I want to live a quiet life. Got it?"

Ann drew her brows together into a deep scowl. "I know that's what you want, but I'm afraid the media doesn't give a fig about your wishes. That's why this idea is so fantastic. Don't say no. As a matter of fact, don't say anything until you've heard me out and given it some thought."

She leaned back against the couch and folded her arms across her chest. "Okay, I'll listen, but that's all. You're not going to convince me to do anything."

Ann grinned, exposing the gap between her two front teeth. "Fair enough." She tucked one leg up under her and faced Melody. "I was skeptical too when I took the call. I mean, who would want to star in a reality show? Especially one where twenty gorgeous guys are vying for your love? But think about it, Mel. The producers screen these guys. They do extensive background checks. We're not talking average Joes here. These guys are the crème de la crème. So aside from having a fabulous time with twenty hunks wining and dining you, we'll put an end to these." Ann held up the pile of messages from the litany of men wishing to meet Melody.

"I'm afraid I'm not getting it. How is my going on *Dream Girl* going to put an end to all this?"

Ann rolled her eyes as if Melody was dense. "It's simple, really. The purpose of the show is for you to find your soul mate, and that's exactly what you're going to do."

"Have you lost your mind? You know how I feel about those shows. They might be fun to watch, but I don't believe anyone there really finds a lasting love."

Ann took hold of her hands and squeezed. "No, silly. I don't believe that either. You only have to give the appearance of falling in love. Whichever man you choose, you announce your engagement to the world. A very long engagement," she said with a wink.

Melody's eyes widened. "I get you now. It's all for show, but as far as the public is concerned, I'm off the market."

"Precisely."

"Oh, Ann. I don't know. It sounds good in theory, but what about the poor man? The one I choose. It's not fair to deceive him."

"Mel, you're such a softy. You're worried about the feelings of a man you don't even know. Toughen up, girl, and worry about yourself."

She shook her head. "Even if I agreed to do it, I don't think I could carry it off. He'd see right through me and know my feelings weren't real. You know I'm a terrible actress."

Ann opened her mouth, then snapped it shut as Mags and Billy entered the room, carrying trays filled with food and drinks.

"Hey guys, what's up?" Billy asked, pushing the papers aside to set her tray down next to the chips and dip. "I've got a bunch of messages for you too, Mel." She reached into her pocket and pulled out a handful.

Mags laughed, though she sounded uneasy. "I do too. Looks like we're going to have to get an unlisted number."

Melody looked at each of her friends. Despite their joking, her newfound celebrity had become quite an imposition. They couldn't continue to live this way. Something had to be done and soon.

She took a deep breath and let it out slowly. Ann's solution was the only one she had. Spending a few weeks with twenty handsome bachelors sure beat disappearing into anonymity, or losing her friends because of this annoying, unwanted celebrity. If she was going to be a media darling, she might as well play the game and get the media to work for her. An island vacation. Fun times with guys who were undoubtedly searching for their fifteen minutes of fame more than true love, anyhow. No one would get hurt, and she'd be off the hook. *Go for it*, that little voice of intuition whispered. Grinning, she said, "Ann, I think you may have come up with the answer after all."

℘℧

Guystof paced his bedroom floor. The clock was ticking, and as each day passed, so did his chances of fulfilling his father's ultimatum. He had to find a bride, no matter how distasteful that might be. But how was he to find one with a huge fortune and do so in a short period of time?

He crossed the room and grabbed his father's letter, then tore it into tiny pieces, letting them flutter to the floor. Impossible. And not only did Father know that, but Theo did as well. The thought of his brother as head of the LeBreque family turned his stomach. Theo was cruel, even by vampire standards, and to have him running things sent a chill straight to Guystof's heart. There had to be a way for him to find a rich woman to marry…

The knock on his door turned his thoughts from his dilemma, at least temporarily. The heavy wooden door opened, and Blakesley, his butler and confidant, strolled in carrying a silver tray topped with a tea set and the morning newspaper. "I thought you might like something warm to drink before you retire for the day, sir."

"That's very thoughtful of you," he replied, offering up a woeful smile. "But sleep is not something I've had much of lately."

"I know that, sir. It shows on your face, especially in the dark rings beneath your eyes. Perhaps if you read a bit, it will take your mind off your problems and help you to relax." Blakesley set the tray on the bedside table and poured a steaming cup of tea, then pulled down the bedspread and proceeded to shut the heavy velvet draperies surrounding the large mahogany four-poster.

Guystof watched as the elderly gentleman with his thinning crop of salt-and-pepper hair and faded hazel eyes tried to make him comfortable. Blakesley's efforts were well appreciated.

He took a careful sip of tea, then picked up the newspaper. It was turned to the Entertainment section. The woman gracing the front page was a beauty. Even on cheap newsprint, there was no denying her classic good looks, but it was the heading, "Multimillionaire to be New Dream Girl," that caught his attention first.

"You sly devil." He laughed, slapping the newspaper on the edge of the table and shifting his gaze to Blakesley, who was trying to creep from the room unnoticed.

With a hand on the doorknob, his butler turned to face him. "Sir? Were you referring to me?"

Guystof let out a chuckle from deep in his belly. "I'm amazed at how clever you are."

Blakesley lifted a bushy white brow. "And how's that, sir?"

"Don't be coy, old man. You set me up to read this." Guystof waved the newspaper in front of him. "Though it's a splendid idea, it's a gamble. Even if the producers select me, there's no guarantee I'll win the Dream Girl's heart."

Blakesley crossed the room in his stilted gait to stand before him. "I've no doubt she'll fall in love with you, sir. None at all. For centuries women have been pursuing you. It's been you, sir, who has not been interested."

"But if this one was to select someone other than me, I'd have used up all my time, giving Theo control."

"You'll not let that happen, Count."

Guystof smiled and rubbed his square jaw line with his fingertips. "Ah, perhaps she will be impressed with the title. What American woman wouldn't love to become a countess, eh, Blakes?"

"Indeed, sir. Indeed."

"It's settled, then. Call the show's producers."

CHAPTER TWO

M elody swallowed the aspirin, then gently laid her throbbing skull back on the couch cushions and groaned. Last night's farewell dinner had been a tearful event, and she'd wound up drinking more than she'd planned. One glass of wine with her meal had been her intention, but whenever her glass went below half full, someone would refill it, then offer up a toast. How could she refuse? Her friends and family had been so wonderful. Not only had they planned the dinner, but they put together a slide show of Fiji, the South Pacific island where *Dream Girl* would be taped. Her mother had done most of the work. No surprise. She owned a travel agency and was a control freak. Athena Johnson's need to run her family's lives may have led to her divorce, but Melody, her only child, was a devoted daughter.

Although Melody would have preferred to curl up in bed with a book, she was a good sport and went along with the whole party thing—even wore a gaudy purple-and-red plastic lei and chowed down on pineapple and roast pig. It wasn't until Mags, Billy, and Ann kicked off their shoes to do a traditional island dance that things started to get out of control. Her father, a normally reserved accountant, had way too much to drink. She understood he was nervous about his baby girl traveling so far away, but dancing on the table was not a good thing. And then when Mom tried to pull him off and knocked the strawberry cream cake onto the floor instead, it was time to leave. And fast. Before the staff at La Folay threw everyone out.

There were plenty of hugs, kisses, and tears, and Melody couldn't wait to get home. Once inside the tranquil walls of her apartment, she wondered if she was doing the right thing. Fiji was so far way. She might as well be going to the moon. And that feeling of dread had not gone away.

She'd tossed and turned all night, and as the pounding in her head increased, so did her fear. Starring in a reality show. Had she lost her mind? Twenty gorgeous guys would soon be vying for her love and attention. How would she cope? A blind date was enough to send her into panic mode, but twenty dates? And on national television? She squeezed her eyes shut to keep the room from spinning. Bile rose up in her throat, and she swallowed hard.

"Coool! Did you know that Fiji lies in the heart of the Pacific Ocean, halfway between the Equator and the South Pole?" The sound of Ann's voice took her mind off her misery, at least temporarily.

"Uh-huh." Melody opened her eyes and looked over at her best friend curled up on the easy chair across the room. With straight brown hair, pecan-colored eyes, freckled skin and a love for neutral-colored clothes, Ann was as nondescript as one could get, but she had more heart than anyone Melody had ever known.

"And did you know that it's home to six species of bats?" Ann held a travelogue of the island on her lap.

"And I need to know that because…?"

"Because it's interesting. Mel, you're going to a beautiful tropical island halfway around the world. Imagine white sandy beaches, crystal-clear azure water, the gentle breeze blowing over your sun-bronzed skin. And I'll be here in Hope, taking my wool sweaters out of mothballs. It might only be September, but winter will be here too soon for my liking."

"I'd be happy to let you go in my place."

Ann raised an eyebrow at her. "Don't be ridiculous. You know I can't do that. Besides, once you get there, I'm sure you're going to love it. Just watch out for the cannibals."

The thought of people eating other people made her stomach churn, and Melody clamped her hand over her mouth.

Ann giggled. "Sorry. Didn't mean to gross you out. And by the way, that practice ended a long time ago."

"Thanks. I feel much better now."

Her friend uncurled her long thin legs and bounded across the room like a rambunctious puppy. She plopped down next to Melody on the couch. "I can't believe you're leaving tomorrow. I know you'll only be gone a few months, but I'm going to miss you so much."

A lump formed in Melody's throat, making it difficult to speak. She fought hard to keep the tears clouding her eyes from spilling onto her cheeks. She mustn't cry. She'd done enough of that last night. As she took a deep breath and swallowed, she tried to think happy thoughts.

"I'll be back home before you know it. You'll see." Melody wasn't sure if she'd succeeded in cheering up Ann, but she still felt awful.

"I want you to have this." Ann reached behind her neck and undid the clasp to the tiny gold cross she always wore. Though both girls were Christians, Ann attended church weekly, while Melody was less regular. Christmas, Easter, and a Sunday or two sprinkled in between.

She pushed Ann's hand away. "I couldn't," she sputtered. "I can't take that from you." Ann's dad had been killed in a car accident when she was a little girl. It was the last thing he'd given to her.

"Okay, then, if you won't keep it, just borrow it. Wear it till you come back." Ann draped it around Melody's neck and clasped it shut. "I don't know why. Maybe it's because we were talking about cannibals, but it'll make me happy knowing you'll have it on."

Melody hugged Ann tightly. She couldn't have asked for a more considerate friend. And she had to admit, she was beginning to feel a bit better.

ഇൽ

Blakesley's intent stare was disconcerting. "I do believe I've come to like your new look, sir."

Guystof gingerly touched his newly cropped, spiky hair. He'd worn it shoulder-length for hundreds of years, and the gelled hairdo felt unnatural. Perhaps stepping out of his seventeenth-century comfort zone wouldn't be as easy as he'd anticipated. Certainly he didn't look forward to donning his modern attire. Cargo pants and Birkenstocks lay at the opposite end of the fashion spectrum from his customary Armani ensembles.

The first thing he'd done after arriving in New York City was to update his appearance. That meant a shopping spree through Bergdorf Goodman and an appointment with Dominick, the city's premier hairstylist. A necessary evil if he was to become one of the bachelors on *Dream Girl*. And his transformation had done the trick. The producers' decision to choose him had been unanimous. He'd left Tristate Studios with a plane ticket for Fiji.

Guystof had one day to perfect his image; then he was off to a tropical island paradise to meet the woman he needed to make fall in love with him. That would be quite a task. He knew nothing of modern American women, but he knew one thing: he'd have to be comfortable in his own skin if he was to succeed. And that meant getting used to jeans. With a tug at his crotch, he pulled his pants down a bit and let out a sigh of relief. Denim would take some getting used to.

Guystof walked over to the window and looked out at the vast array of skyscrapers—all glass and steel sparkling like giant crystals. The view from the forty-second floor of the New York Hilton was spectacular.

The bright afternoon sun warmed his face, and he smiled. No need to hide from its rays now. He twisted the gold crested ring he wore on his right hand. Beneath the LeBreque shield was a tiny vial given to him by Blakesley. It held enough potion to keep him human for the duration of the show. One drop daily was all he needed to suppress his hunger for blood. He could do all the things mortals could, and that included enjoying the sunlight. But, as with anything that seemed too good to be true, there were drawbacks. Too much of the potion could be disastrous. Its side effects were unknown. Ambrus, his grandfather and a very fine sorcerer, had conjured the potion back in the sixteenth century in the hopes of reversing the curse that had turned his family into vampires, but he was burned at the stake before he'd finished testing it. Luckily, he'd entrusted it to Blakesley for safekeeping.

Guystof couldn't worry about the potion's dangers now. This was his only opportunity to compete with the other bachelors on an even playing field. Being a vampire had too many disadvantages. And if he hoped to win, he had to appear as human as the next guy.

Guystof turned his back to the sun and looked across the room to his companion. He would miss the old man. Although Blakesley couldn't accompany him on his trip, he might be able to serve him in other ways. "Keep an eye on Theo, will you?"

Blakesley chuckled. "Don't trust your brother?"

"I'd be a fool if I did."

"No need to worry, sir. You can count on me."

Guystof crossed the room in three long strides. He stood beside Blakesley and clamped his hand on the old man's shoulder. "I know I can. You know as well as I how important this game is."

⁝⁞

When the white stretch limo sent by Tristate Studios to take Melody to the airport parked in front of her townhouse, it seemed like the whole neighborhood lined up on the sidewalk for a look.

"Excuse me." She wove through the crowd, pulling her new lime-green paisley luggage behind her. Not exactly her first choice, but Ann had suggested she buy the brightly colored paisley instead of the basic black Melody had preferred, insisting she'd have a much easier time finding it at the airport baggage claim. There was no doubting that.

The limo driver slid out from behind the wheel and headed toward her. A distinguished gentleman she guessed to be in his mid-fifties, he carried himself with an air that said he was used to working for the very wealthy. Why, with his navy suit accented by lots of shiny brass buttons, he was better dressed than she. Melody glanced down at her favorite brown slacks and plain white blouse and frowned. She felt very much like the librarian she'd always wanted to be, rather than the multimillionaire she'd become. His cool gray eyes gave her the once over, but his expression remained politely aloof.

"Hello, Miss Johnson. My name is Rupert. I hope your trip to the airport will be a pleasant one." He swung open the passenger door and held his hand out to her.

Before accepting his assistance, she turned to her roommates. Mags and Billy were trying hard to cover their sadness with the phoniest smiles she'd ever seen, while Ann had her face buried in Gizmo's fur as she struggled to keep the pug from leaping out of her arms and into Melody's.

Despite her best effort, her bottom lip quivered. "Come on you guys, cheer up. I'll be back before you know it."

"Have a safe trip," they chimed.

Not wanting to prolong the good-byes, she gave Gizmo a kiss on the head, then took Rupert's hand and stepped into the limo. He closed the door, then loaded her luggage into the trunk. She leaned back against the glove-soft seat, inhaling the rich perfume of fine leather and exotic wood.

"It's hard to leave loved ones, isn't it?"

Startled to discover she wasn't alone, Melody flicked a tear from her eye before turning to the woman seated in the far corner across from her. Judging by her eclectic mix of clothing, the woman had a hard time choosing from which decade to dress. She wore white fishnet stockings, a mini skirt short enough to be X-rated, silver stiletto heels and a low-cut knit shirt that did little to conceal breasts too perfect not to have been shaped by some high-priced plastic surgeon. Bright red hair with glints of copper swirled eighties-style big around her narrow face. And her makeup. Way too much makeup. Granted, Melody was the natural type, but even she knew the woman had gone too far. When she smiled, a smear of lipstick coated one front tooth.

"Join me in a glass of champagne?" she asked, handing Melody a fluted crystal goblet.

She shook her head. What she didn't need was alcohol. "I don't mean to be rude, but who are you? I wasn't told I'd have a traveling companion."

The woman giggled, then took a gulp of champagne, looking at Melody through the bubbles. "I'm your hairdresser and makeup artist, silly. And, boy, am I an artiste. The studio thought you'd be more comfortable with a little friendly female companionship."

Melody raised her eyebrows in surprise and held out her hand. "Melody Johnson. Pleasure to meet you."

The woman fumbled with the champagne glass, nearly spilling it on her lap when she tried to shake Melody's hand. "Sugar."

Of course that was her name. It suited her perfectly. Melody turned to look out the rearview mirror and caught one last glance of her home before it faded into the distance. It was too late to turn back now.

Shifting her gaze back to Sugar, Melody took a deep breath and smiled. She seemed nice enough, and at least Melody didn't have to feel out of place around her. The woman's sense of style was worse than her own.

"I've got butterflies in my stomach," Sugar confessed. "I've never been on a plane before." She took a long drink of champagne, and Melody noticed her hand shook.

Great. With her own nervousness threatening to swamp her, the thought of traveling with another novice flier did nothing to ease her mind. She hoped the combination of nerves and champagne didn't wind up making Sugar sick. "Have you worked for Tristate long?" she asked.

"This is my first gig." Sugar must have noticed Melody's look of shock, for she reached over and patted her hands. "Don't worry, hon, I've been in the business for years. Just never worked for a big TV studio before. My days were spent behind a chair. I've worked on famous people, though. Mostly models. You know Jasmine Loka?"

Melody nodded. "I've seen her in magazines."

"Yeah. She's real famous. I do her hair." Sugar nearly beamed with pride. "So it was a no-brainer for my friend Angela, who's due to have a baby any day now, and I sure hope it's soon cause she looks about ready to burst, to recommend me for the Fiji shoot. I mean, Angela's been working for Tristate forever, and she's real good, but nobody's better than Sugar."

Melody hoped Sugar's talent matched her ego. "I'm very pleased you're here," she said with a forced smile, then closed her eyes. She could feel a headache coming on. Melody knew it was nerves. She needed to relax, and the best way for her to do that was with a good book. Unfortunately, she'd packed her reading material in her tote in the limo's trunk, so maybe she could doze a little instead. The ride to the airport wasn't long, about an hour, but any amount of time worry-free would be a welcome relief.

What seemed like seconds later, she felt a jab in her ribs—Sugar's elbow.

"Wake up, hon. We're here." Sugar bounced on the seat like an excited child.

Melody glanced out the window as the limo pulled up to the United terminal. JFK swarmed with people. Rupert came around to open her door, but without waiting for assistance, Sugar bolted out the other side and proceeded to yank luggage out of the trunk. The way she manhandled their bags, Melody had visions of them popping open and their clothes strewn everywhere. Luckily, an airport employee took over for her.

After thanking Rupert and watching the limo weave in and out of traffic as it roared away, she followed their mountain of luggage to check-in. Sugar jostled ahead in line with her airline ticket in hand. Melody fumbled through her purse for hers. From the corner of her eye, she noticed an extremely handsome man watching her. She hugged her shoulder bag closer to her body. Hadn't Mags warned her about purse-snatchers targeting women traveling alone? Melody edged closer to Sugar—as if the perky bombshell would provide any protection. Still, better than nothing.

"We made great time. There's more than two hours till our flight leaves," Melody said, glancing at her watch.

"Good. We can freshen up and find somewhere to buy a pack of gum. I hear chewing helps to keep your ears from popping."

Trying to remain inconspicuous, Melody pretended to flick a piece of lint from her pants in order to catch a glimpse off to her right, where the handsome stranger had been standing. Shoot! He caught her staring. Maybe he didn't want her purse, but her. Her cheeks grew hot. He must have recognized her. He could be one of those persistent gold-diggers. She tapped her foot impatiently. Why wasn't this line moving more quickly?

The gorgeous man retrieved two bags from the same airport employee who had handled her luggage. He reached into the pocket of khaki trousers that hugged his thighs perfectly and pulled out his wallet, tipped the man, then took his place in line.

Well, how much more paranoid could she be? The man had been waiting for his luggage, that's all. Okay, he'd obviously been checking her out, but so what? Men had been admiring women for centuries. She had to stop thinking everyone who looked at her wanted her money. Maybe she needed this vacation far away from New York more than she'd realized. At least in Fiji, there'd be no need to look over her shoulder and wonder who might be watching her, wondering if she was the lucky woman who'd just won a fortune. The men on *Dream Girl* would be there for a different reason—to find true love or to find fame. Sure, they knew her story, and her bank balance. But they didn't need her money.

Each man could brag of his own success. She'd been briefed by the show's producers on the bachelors they'd selected for her. Her bachelors included a millionaire businessman, a professional football player, a doctor, even a European count. Men she'd never have met in her previous incarnation as an impoverished librarian. Melody straightened her shoulders and moved ahead in line. Maybe, just maybe, she would find her soul mate. She hardly dared let herself think that way, but why not? Stranger things had happened—like a small town girl winning the lottery and getting on a reality TV show, for instance. Somewhere in the world, her true love waited. She just had to find him. For all she knew, he could be the handsome man who'd just been admiring her.

Unfortunately, bachelor number one must have lost interest already. He gazed steadily ahead and not at her. Melody studied him covertly. Did he have a girlfriend? Maybe even a wife and kids. Sugar's pointy elbow in her side jagged her back to reality.

"You're next, hon," her busty companion said.

The airline attendant scowled at her, clearly not pleased that she'd held up the line. "Miss! Ticket, please."

"Oops, sorry, daydreaming." At the same time Melody plopped her paperwork down, Ann's gold cross fell off her neck and onto the counter. She quickly scooped it up, dropped it in her purse and made a mental note to check the clasp. If it had fallen off elsewhere, it probably would have been lost.

She was whisked through the check-in process with plenty of time to kill before their flight was called, so they decided to look for a ladies room, then a place where Sugar could buy gum. Melody cast a quick glance over her shoulder to the handsome stranger, but he stood at the counter engrossed in airline business. She'd never see him again. An unexpected pang of regret tightened her belly. Just as quickly, she shrugged it off. Talk about the world's fastest infatuation! Dream Girl's man-hunting premise must be rubbing off on her.

When they located their gate, Melody was more than ready to spend the rest of the time reading. Sugar liked to talk, and she'd been chattering nonstop about the salon industry. Melody had learned more than she needed to know about perms and hair color. She settled into a chair and pulled a book out of her tote before placing the canvas bag on the floor.

Sugar turned to her and blew a big pink bubble from between her fire engine red lips. The bubble popped and Sugar grinned. "If you don't mind, hon, I'm gonna go hang out by the window and look at the planes."

Melody nodded. Thankful for a little quiet time, she slipped on her reading glasses and buried her nose in her book. But she'd barely cracked the cover when footsteps sounded behind her.

"Do you mind if I sit here?"

The thick, European, and utterly delicious accent poured into Melody's ears. She looked up into the deepest chocolate eyes she'd ever seen. A rush of recognition jolted her from her book. The handsome stranger from check-in. Of average height, his thickly muscled physique was anything but average. His ash-blond curls fell over his forehead, shading finely sculptured features. His full, sensuous lips curved in the hint of a smile, and Melody had to make it a point not to stare. "Handsome" didn't do him justice; "beautiful" came closer.

She whipped off her glasses and kicked her tote out of his way. "Please...sit."

"Thank you. I hope I'm not interrupting your reading." As he sat beside her, he leaned over to see the title of her book. The heady scent of spice infiltrated her nose. "*Wuthering Heights.* Ah, wonderful choice. I'm quite a fan of Catherine, as I'm sure you are of Heathcliff?"

Forget Heathcliff. I'm a fan of yours. "I love the classics." She hoped he didn't see her trembling fingers when she closed the book and, along with her glasses, popped it back into her tote.

"I couldn't help but notice you in line earlier. Your luggage caught my eye."

Her luggage. Her lime-green paisley luggage had attracted this hunk. Not her money, or her looks. She wanted to laugh out loud.

Instead, she retained her composure and smiled sweetly. "That was my friend's idea."

"Interesting choice. I like it."

Melody would have to make it a point to thank Ann for her odd taste. "Are you on this flight?"

"I have some business in Los Angeles. And you?"

"I have a layover at LAX and one in New Zealand, then it's on to Fiji."

"Where's your husband? He's not joining you on such a romantic vacation?"

Oh, what a line! But coming from him it was more of a turn-on than a turn-off. A giggle escaped from between her lips, and she felt like a silly schoolgirl. "No, no husband. Just my…friend…over there." She looked at Sugar, who stood by the window in all her New Jersey prom-queen glory.

He raised a brow and politely made no comment. "Ah, well, perhaps you'll find the man of your dreams while in paradise."

Maybe I've already found him. "Hmmm, perhaps. I guess you never know where you might find your soul mate. It could even happen at an airport." Did she just say that? Oh Lord! Her face burned, and she knew it had to be scarlet. She wanted to crawl under her seat, or, better yet, die from embarrassment.

But he smiled, exposing a row of even white teeth. "Yes, it might happen at an airport. Maybe even this one… Maybe even today."

This couldn't be happening. She shouldn't be flirting when even now the jet rumbled on the tarmac, ready to whisk her into the arms of her dream man. But it seemed forever since she'd been attracted to anyone. Not since she'd dated Greg Sinclair in college. The jock and party boy had done a good job of turning her off to men… At least that type of man. Their brief two-month relationship, if you could call it that, ended abruptly when he told her she was boring.

The real problem—for him—boiled down to her refusal to sleep with him. Greg's rejection had hurt nonetheless. It seemed her ideal man lived between the pages of her books. The classic heroes who existed only on paper—or apparently, appeared in airports. And the way this hot guy's striking dark eyes delved into her own made her want to say, *The heck with Fiji, I've found my man at the United terminal.* Her breath hitched as she envisioned a night of wild, passionate love. She knotted her hands in her lap and tried to control her emotions. What in the world had come over her? She had to stop thinking such thoughts. She was a nice girl.

"Your accent... Is it German?" she asked, quickly changing the subject.

"Romanian."

"Oh. I've never met anyone from Romania before, not that I've met many Germans, either."

He laughed, a rich, hearty sound that set her pulse drumming. "There aren't many of my kind who've ventured into this part of the world. They're mainly still in Europe. Though I'm sure if they knew what your country was like and the people...the women"—his glance traveled over her, lingering on her lips— "they would come to America."

Okay. She had to get a grip. Her libido had her head spinning and heat thrumming through her veins. "What type of business are you in?"

"I draw blood."

Her brow wrinkled before she realized what he must have meant. "You're a phlebotomist? I'll bet you need a strong stomach to do that type of work."

"I don't mind the sight of blood."

"Ick. A paper cut makes me feel faint."

He chuckled, then reached for her hand. Cool, almost cold,

fingers twined around her hot, sweaty ones. His smooth lips brushed the back of her hand. Oh, to feel those velvet lips elsewhere, in other places... A tremor of lust tumbled through her.

"It was a pleasure talking with you."

And you too, Melody thought. He could read her the phone book in that thick, sexy accent and she'd be one happy woman.

He rose gracefully and smiled down at her. "Perhaps we'll meet again."

Melody blinked and he—simply vanished. Where did he go? Frantically, she scanned the crowd forming around her gate. Gone without a trace. How could that be? He couldn't just disappear into thin air. *Do something!* "Don't go," she called. "I don't even know your name."

The airport intercom drowned her words. "All business class passengers traveling on flight 132, please board the airplane now."

Sugar galloped over to her, clearly anxious to see the inside of the plane. "That's us, hon. Let's go." But when she saw the look on Melody's face, she stopped walking. "What's wrong? Are you sick?"

Definitely. Heartsick. "I—ah, did you see the good looking blond man I was talking to?"

Sugar's pencil-thin eyebrows lifted. "No, sweetie. I didn't see you with anyone. But you could bet if I'd known you were with some hot guy, I'd have been right by your side." She giggled. "Screw looking at the planes."

"Well, he was here." She touched the chair next to her, where just a few moments ago he'd sat. It was as cool as his fingers. "And then he was gone."

"I don't know what to tell you, except we've got to go." Sugar grabbed her arm and pulled her toward the gate. "Look, sweetie, you're bound to see him again if he's on this flight, right?"

"I suppose." Melody nearly collided into the back of an elderly woman as she searched for a glimpse of curly ash-blond hair.

"Sorry." Wow, that guy had really tilted her world. She stepped around the old woman, handed her boarding pass to the attendant and followed Sugar onto the plane. It wasn't until they were settled in their seats that Melody's racing heart slowed to a normal rhythm. Whatever spell she'd been under finally began to fade and reality roared back like the growling jet engines. Sure, the romantic Romanian had been charismatic, but the men she would meet in Fiji were bound to be just as suave. And who knew, maybe one would make her heart pound even faster than had the man with the dreamy chocolate eyes.

⁊⌣

Theo arrived in Los Angeles by the only method he knew would avoid jetlag—magic. Disappearing and reappearing somewhere else was a specialty of his. As he drank in his first breath of the sultry California breeze whispering through the hotel window, he scanned the hallway to confirm no wayward maid or hotel patron had witnessed his remarkable arrival. He had half a day's advance on his brother, thanks to his gift. The sorcery on his father's side of the family mated with his mother's witchcraft proved a potent combination. Not all vampires possessed his talent. Fortunately for Theo, Guystof hadn't been so lucky. His mother had been a mere mortal with no special powers whatsoever. Though Guystof could perform a trick or two when need be, he was no match for Theo.

Such a shame too, especially for the lovely Melody. He hoped to add her to his harem of pretty, young vampires. The thought of her sweet, soft flesh, her long graceful neck, made his fangs begin to protrude. *Careful. You mustn't get sidetracked. You've a job to do. She'll be yours soon enough.*

With a deep breath, he concentrated on the task at hand— Johnny Evans, poet and philosophy professor at Berkeley, thirty years old, a bachelor on *Dream Girl*, and the perfect candidate to do Theo's bidding.

Standing in Johnny's bedroom doorway, Theo watched him sleep. The bachelor's chest rattled, and he let out a loud snore. Theo would have to do something about that undesirable trait. He crossed the room and stood beside the bed, placing his hand over the man's face until his breathing came out in a soft puff.

Moonlight poured in through the window, lighting Johnny's features. Handsome and rugged, he had thick chestnut hair and a heavily muscled physique. Melody was sure to find him attractive, and with the personality Theo was about to give him, Johnny would be irresistible.

He bent down and blew in the bachelor's ear. The man twitched but did not awaken. "When you rise," Theo whispered, "you shall exude charisma and sex appeal. And you'll do anything to win Melody Johnson's love."

He watched Johnny for a few more seconds, fighting the growing urge to sink his fangs into the man's neck. He couldn't give in to his hunger now. Johnny Evans' importance as a pawn far outweighed his appeal as dinner. He was the decoy that would keep Guystof from his chosen bride.

Though his brother's magic didn't rival his own, Guystof could be very charming. And with Melody's love of dark, brooding heroes, she was bound to find him hard to resist. Precisely why Theo had to intervene.

CHAPTER THREE

Melody stared out the Island Hopper's window. The helicopter provided a fast scenic ride from the Nadi Airport on the main island of Viti Levu to Taveuni, the third largest island in Fiji. She sucked in her breath at the beauty below. The island sparkled like a magnificent gem. The beach—a golden bronze—lay in contrast to the glistening blue of the Pacific Ocean. This was a long way from her small rural hometown. She felt the need to pinch herself to prove this all wasn't just a dream.

Sugar squeezed her hand, her mouth open in awe. "I've never seen nothing like this."

"Ladies, you're about to enter paradise," the pilot said with a smile.

A few minutes later, the helicopter set down on the crosshairs of a landing pad. The huge, thumping rotors kicked up a storm of dust before they slowed enough for Melody and Sugar to hop out. A car waited at the airport. Not a limo, but a nice, clean sedan that would carry them to Malaku, the sixty-acre resort where *Dream Girl* would be filmed.

They traveled a dirt road, passing a traditional Fijian village set amongst the deep vegetation of the jungle, before reaching their destination. Despite the heat, Melody shivered as her imagination conjured up images of cannibals hiding within the dark, green foliage.

She remembered Ann telling her from the travelogue that Malaku had once been a coconut plantation and that was evidenced by the rows of lush trees they passed. Up ahead, Melody spotted a large grouping of thatched roof huts. A beautiful woman with long, straight blue-black hair waved to their car. Her grass skirt swayed around her hips as she stepped back so the sedan could park along the curb. Colorful leis made from native island flowers hung from her arms, and when Melody and Sugar stepped out of the car, she draped one around each of their necks.

Sugar held the fragrant petals of the lei up to her nose, inhaled deeply, then sneezed. "I hope I'm not allergic," she said between sniffles.

Melody ran her thumb over the velvety flowers. "You probably got nectar up your nose, that's all," she said, not wanting to add to Sugar's drama.

"*Ni Sa Bula.*" The native woman smiled, exposing teeth as white as pearls. "Greetings."

"*Ni Sa Bula,*" Melody and Sugar replied.

"If you'll come with me, I'll show you to your *bures.*" She must have noticed their puzzled expressions. "Your houses," she explained.

"Oh, oh, of course." Melody fell in step alongside her, while Sugar tagged behind, more interested in the three young boys who'd emerged from behind a large banana tree and were now struggling to carry their luggage.

"You must be the Dream Girl," the native woman said, her gaze flicking over Melody.

"Yes, I'm Melody Johnson."

"We've all been so anxious to meet you. I'm Serenie LaLe. My family owns Malaku." There was no denying the pride in her tone or the confidence in her stride. And why not? The plantation was beautiful.

Everywhere Melody looked, lush tropical gardens and gorgeous trees with large glossy leaves and big, round green fruit covered the fertile earth. Serenie led her to a secluded *bure* with an ocean view. Built on a cliff edge, it offered a panoramic view that mingled the gardens with the reef. A private path led down the cliff to a beautiful white sand bay, where palm trees overhung the aqua water.

"That's Dolphin Bay," Serenie said, following Melody's stunned gaze.

"I've never seen anything more beautiful."

"And it's yours alone for your entire stay."

"I don't know what to say." Melody looked out over the crystal clear blue water. A sense of peace settled on her as she leaned on the white iron railing and took a deep breath of island air. Paradise! For the first time, she got a sense of what her lottery winnings could buy. Wouldn't it be fun to fly her friends out here too? Once *Dream Girl* ended, she could have Mags, Ann, and Billy join her. They'd lounge on the beach drinking coconut rum and laugh about the quirks of fate that had brought them all together.

"May you find your future husband here," Serenie said in her soft, sweet voice.

A cool trade wind blew across Melody's skin, covering her with fresh ocean air. "I don't believe there's a more romantic place on earth." Then why did she suddenly feel so homesick?

"Let me show you the inside of your *bure*," Serenie said, opening the door.

Melody followed her into the hut. Tropical flowers in full bloom were everywhere. Vases overflowed with orchids, lotus blossoms, birds of paradise, and gardenias, perfuming the house with the scents of white ginger and other exotic spices. Fijian artwork hung on the walls. Carved bowls and pottery covered the windowsills. There was a fully stocked mini-bar on top of which sat a huge wicker basket that overflowed with bananas, pineapples, and papayas. Beside it was the traditional welcome drink of fresh iced coconut juice served in its own shell.

Serenie led the way into the bedroom. A king-size bed covered by a white mosquito net canopy took up most of the room. French doors led the way to a private stonewalled courtyard containing an outside shower, a sundeck and spacious Jacuzzi pool. What a shame Melody wasn't really here to meet the man of her dreams… To be surrounded by such luxury while in the arms of your lover would be heaven on earth.

"I think you'll find your stay here most comfortable," Serenie said with a wink.

"How could I not?" Melody sank onto the bed. A red-and-white flower print sarong draped the headboard. She ran her hand over the soft material.

"That's your *Sulu*. You're to wear it tomorrow when you meet the bachelors. They'll be arriving throughout the day. So you have lots of free time today. You can relax, swim, or take a walk along the beach. But you mustn't leave the private grounds of your *bure*. The producers don't want you meeting any of the bachelors ahead of schedule. Might give someone an unfair advantage."

"Of course."

Melody followed Serenie back into the sitting room, where they nearly ran headfirst into Sugar and the three boys who'd carried their luggage.

Sugar was eating a banana and tossing papayas from the fruit basket to each of the boys. "You don't mind, right, Mel?"

"No, not at all. Help yourselves."

Serenie scowled and yelled something in Fijian at the boys as they grabbed for some pawpaws. "Your work isn't done. You still have more luggage to carry." She cast her glance over to Sugar, then looked apologetically at Melody. "Sometimes my boys forget their manners."

Melody raised a brow. "Those are your boys?" Serenie didn't look much older than a child herself.

The island woman smiled, and a self-conscious blush stole up her face. "It's times like these that make being a widow difficult. I can't say to them, 'Wait till your father gets home.'"

"You have a lovely family, Serenie."

"Thank you, miss. If there's anything you need, please just ask." As she followed her boys out the door, she turned back to Melody. "I almost forgot. Tonight you'll dine with the producers in the large *bure*. It's the first one we passed."

"At what time?" Melody called after her.

"The *lali* drum will inform you when the meal is ready."

Sugar took the last bite of her banana and tossed the peel into the trash. "I'm off too, hon. I'll see you at dinner when the drum beats."

Alone at last, Melody could hardly wait to unpack, shower, and bask in the afternoon sun. In the bathroom, she found coconut soaps, shampoo, conditioner, a hairdryer and a plush terry robe. This was luxury. She hadn't thanked Ann nearly enough for talking her into becoming the Dream Girl. She would make it up to her in a big way.

She let the shower spray pummel her tired muscles until they relaxed and the exhausting thirty-one hour trip was long forgotten. She combed the tangles from her hair, pulled it up into a loose twist, then slipped into her favorite string bikini.

The linen closet was stocked with plenty of towels, and she grabbed one to take with her to the beach. She also took a bottle of sunscreen, the coconut juice drink, and a couple of books about Fijian culture that she'd found on a table. Melody was ready for a wonderful afternoon at the beach—her very own private beach.

She walked down the path to the bay, where the huge palm trees that lined the beach swayed in the breeze. White clouds sailed in the blue sky and the hot sun shone, sparkling the sea like turquoise glass. She spread her towel over the warm sand and lay down on her back. The heat from the sun blended with the cool southeastern breeze, creating the perfect temperature to sunbathe. She closed her eyes, and her thoughts drifted to the ash-blond stranger she'd met at JFK. If only she'd gotten his name or given him her phone number. Although that would have been a bold thing for her to do, it would have been worth it. Now she would never see him again and never know if that initial attraction might have developed into something more, but before her thoughts drifted farther down that path, common sense returned. *Don't be ridiculous. You don't believe in love at first sight.*

Beads of perspiration rolled from her forehead onto her cheeks. She sat up, reached for her coconut juice, and took a sip. As she stared out at the ocean, she blinked quickly. Who was that in amongst the waves? He looked like a Greek god! She must be seeing things, she thought, and squeezed her eyes shut. But when she opened them, there he stood, golden and splendid, his lithe frame shimmering under the tropical sun. He prowled toward her, his spiky hair jet black and his eyes a cool pale blue.

Her mouth went dry, and she gulped down her drink. But the juice did nothing to still the thunderous beat of her heart. This man was Heathcliff and Rhett Butler rolled into one. Okay, maybe she did believe in love at first sight after all.

ഇന്റെ

It took Guystof no time at all to realize the gorgeous woman on the beach in the hot-pink string bikini was Melody Johnson. As he strode toward her, he couldn't believe his good fortune. The tide must have carried him farther than he'd thought. Glancing over his shoulder at the bachelors' huts way off in the distance, he noticed they were little more than specks set amongst the heavy vegetation of the island.

Meeting Melody before tomorrow's scheduled introductions might prove to be the edge he'd hoped for. Now all he had to do was charm her, and he could be well on his way to winning the heart of his future bride.

More lovely than her photo, Melody appeared like a mirage against the miles of iridescent beach. Her peaches and cream skin was tinged with red along the edges of her bikini, the base of her neck, and the tip of her small upturned nose.

"Looks like you need more sunblock," Guystof said, coming across the hot sand to stand before her.

"Excuse me?" She used her hand to shield her bluer than blue eyes from the sun as she peered up at him.

"You're beginning to burn."

"Oh!" She lifted her bathing suit strap and looked at her shoulder. "I haven't even been out that long." Her voice was tinged with regret, as if now she'd be forced to go inside. "No matter what I do, I always seem to burn before I tan." Her gaze shifted back to him, lingering on his bronzed chest. "I don't suppose you have that problem."

No need for her to know he was a novice in the sunbathing department. Blakesley's insistence that he use an indoor tanning lotion seemed to have worked, giving the impression he'd spent weeks in the sun. "I'm Guy LeBreque." Another of Blakesley's ideas was for him to shorten his name to achieve a modern sound. "And you're…?" he asked, feigning ignorance to her identity.

A frown drooped the corners of her perfectly shaped lips.

Sensing her hesitation, he held his hand out to her. "I can assure you, I don't bite."

A hint of a smile brightened her face. "I'm Melody Johnson." Her gaze flicked over the endless expanse of empty beach before she placed her small, warm hand in his.

Two things surprised him: the firmness of her handshake and the incredible softness of her skin. Although petite, she was by no means frail. "It's a pleasure to meet you, Miss Melody Johnson."

She seemed to relax some, but still appeared uneasy. Was there something about him that made her uncomfortable? He'd taken his daily dose of the potion, so he should appear as human as she.

"You're one of the bachelors, aren't you?"

"Yes." *And you're most definitely a Dream Girl.* He dropped his gaze, letting it travel slowly over her slim body, lingering a little at where her breasts nicely filled out her bikini top, and at the rounded curve of her hips, but not too long so as to be rude. Her skin blushed to a lovely shade of rose while he openly admired her.

"You shouldn't be here." Her voice rose an octave.

He lifted a brow. "And why's that?"

"It's against the rules."

"Really?" He reclined beside her, crowding her on the big white beach towel, the edge of his wet swim trunks brushing the side of her thigh. "And what rules are those?"

"This beach is private. You're not supposed to be here. Not supposed to meet me… Not until tomorrow." She curled her toes into the sand and bit her lip, but she didn't kick him off her towel or demand that he leave.

Guystof propped himself up on one elbow and smiled. "Well, the damage is already done, and no harm has come to you."

She set the drink she'd been holding down on the towel and shook her finger at him. "I'm serious. If the producers find out...well, I don't know what might happen. They just might boot you off the show."

He tried hard not to laugh. She certainly was a feisty little thing. "Don't you think that would be a tad extreme?"

"Not if they thought you'd gained an unfair advantage over the other men."

"And what do you think, Melody? Have I?" he asked in his sexiest tone.

Her delicate brow furrowed. "What kind of question is that? I've only just met you and I know nothing about—"

He leaned over and pressed his mouth against hers, cutting off her words. Her petal-soft lips parted beneath his gentle but insistent pressure, and the fragrant aroma of musk, sandalwood and amber surrounded him. Her back stiffened, he was sure from shock, but then he felt her surrender to his deepening kiss. Draping an arm across her shoulders, he pulled her nearer, so that the wild pounding of her heart mingled with his own. As she began to melt against him, he pulled back. She stared with glazed eyes into his. Her breasts rose and fell in a deep sigh beneath the deliciously skimpy bikini top.

"What do you think now, Melody?" His words rolled off his tongue in the deep Romanian accent he worked so hard to conceal. "Now that you know how I kiss..."

She blinked quickly and shook her head as if what had just happened had been a dream. "I-I-I don't know," she stuttered and ran her fingertip over her lips. "I don't know what to think, other than you're awfully bold." Melody scooted across the towel so that at least a foot separated them.

"Perhaps, but you can't deny that you enjoyed our kiss as much as I," he said with a wicked grin.

She planted her hands on her hips. "I didn't kiss you. I don't kiss men I don't know. You kissed me."

"You may not have initiated it, but I know when a woman responds to me. And you, darling, were on fire."

Her eyes smoldered to almost black. "Why you arrogant—"

"Careful," he interrupted. "You might hurt my feelings. I'm really quite sensitive."

"I doubt that," she muttered beneath her breath. "Is that how men behave where you come from?"

A chuckle rose from deep in his belly. "My dear, some are much worse than I." An image of Theo came to mind, clouding the otherwise sunny day.

"And where exactly do you come from?" she asked. "I know I've heard that accent before."

"Moldavia."

"Romania?"

He nodded.

She studied him closely, as if there was something familiar about him. "Huh, I've never met anyone from that part of the world before, and now I've met two."

The blood pulsed through Guystof's temples. He struggled to keep his expression composed. "Really? And where did you meet the other?"

"At JFK, while waiting for my flight. He seemed really nice but disappeared before I could even get his name. Maybe you know him. He has curly blond hair…"

A dreamy look came into her eyes, and Guystof's stomach churned. "Sorry, I'm afraid I don't know who that might have been." He had no doubt that it was his evil, conniving brother, but he wasn't about to tell Melody that. He should have known the dirty dog would try to prevent him from winning her heart. Well, at least he was familiar with Theo's tricks and would be ready for whatever Theo planned to do from here out.

He reached over and squeezed her hand. "I should go, before someone sees me here with you."

She shaded her eyes again, and the cornflower blue turned sapphire. Her freckled nose wrinkled as she grinned. "I have a feeling this isn't the first time you've broken a rule."

"And probably not the last. I like to win, Melody. And I'll do whatever it takes to get what I want." He held her gaze in an unwavering stare. She looked away first, obviously embarrassed by his intensity.

"I'll see you tomorrow, then," he said as he stood.

She tipped her head, her eyebrows arched in gentle reproach. "Yes, when we'll meet for the first time."

"No need to worry, Melody. I'll never give today away. It'll be our little secret." He turned and walked toward the water, but before diving into the waves, he called over his shoulder to her, "Don't forget the sun block. I don't want my future wife to get burned." His splash covered up her reply, but he didn't need to hear her words to know he'd made a lasting impression on her. And that was just as he'd hoped. What he hadn't planned on, though, was what he'd felt for her. He'd expected her to be beautiful, but he'd had no idea how wonderful she'd feel in his arms or how his heart would skip a beat when he kissed her.

A deep sadness came over him as he remembered what he was—a blood-sucking monster not all that different from his brother—and despite the potion's ability to make him appear human, its effects were temporary. Nothing would alter what he was or what he ultimately had to do. And if he didn't keep his emotions at bay, it would only make it more difficult when the time came for him to end Melody's mortal life.

꽁꿍

Melody watched Guy disappear amongst the waves. The man was incorrigible. She ran her fingertip over her lips—where just a few minutes ago his kiss had left her breathless. She'd never been kissed like *that* before. And by a stranger. What had she been thinking to allow him to do that?

She gathered up her belongings and marched back to her *bure,* as angry with herself as she was with him. The next time she saw him, she'd better be cool and distant. There were nineteen other bachelors for her to meet, and if they were anything like Guy, she was in trouble. Her hormones were raging like a sixteen-year-old's.

Melody set the coconut drink on the bar, dropped the books on a chair, and padded toward the bathroom to freshen up. There were no clocks in her *bure* and her watch still showed New York time, but her internal clock told her it had to be late afternoon. Since she had no idea when dinner was; the only thing she knew was that she'd better be ready when that *lali* drum beat.

The relaxing sound of the Jacuzzi filtered in through the french doors, a reminder that she needn't bathe inside. She hesitated, her reserve holding her back, then smiled and stepped out of her bikini. There was no need to act the part of the uptight librarian here. She could let loose. Melody could become the spontaneous woman she'd always wanted to be. Why, hadn't she already begun her transformation? She'd encountered two gorgeous men and hadn't shrunk away from either one. Quite the opposite. She'd even let one kiss her. And enjoyed it too. Yes, she could have the time of her life here.

She dunked her toe in the spa and sighed deeply. This was indeed paradise. As she sank into the bubbling water, she imagined Guy in the hot tub with her. She envisioned his startling ice-blue eyes—a pale blue as she'd never seen before—locked with hers in a "do I ever want you" stare. She dipped her face in the water and blew out a stream of bubbles. Oh, yeah, he was definitely hot. But despite her physical attraction to him, she needed to remember how arrogant and bold he'd been. Men like that were nothing but trouble. What she should be looking for was a nice, quiet man who shared her love of books. One who would want her more for her mind than for her libido.

She shifted her thoughts away from men and onto what to wear to dinner. An hour later she steadied her trembling hands in the folds of her tangerine silk dress and entered the large *bure* where seated at a round table in the center of the hut sat the *Dream Girl* producers. Although she'd met with them all before, the impact of what they had in store for her hadn't hit home until now. In less than twenty-four hours, the cameras would roll and the taping of *Dream Girl* would begin.

Somewhere not too far away, twenty hunks waited to meet her, hopeful that she'd fall in love and make one her husband. What they didn't know was that she had no intention of doing that. Of course, she hoped to meet the man of her dreams someday, but she had little faith that would happen on network TV. When this was all over, she'd go home to her mundane life and live in peace again. After all, that was why she was here, to rid herself of those bothersome gold-digging men. If she just focused on her objective, maybe she'd forget that thirty million people would be tuning in each week to watch her find her soul mate.

Above her head, paper lanterns hung from the ceiling, casting a golden glow over the faces of the people she was about to dine with. Eddie Hatch, supervising producer and a no-nonsense kind of guy, chatted with Sugar. His gaze kept drifting up to her big hair that swirled like a copper halo around her head. Across from him sat Daniel Stone, the director, and to his right was executive producer

Wendy Jackson, the toughest one in the group. Even Henry Lyons, the show's host, was there. With a deep breath and a firm resolve, Melody stepped up to the table, plastered a smile on her face, and said, "Good evening, everybody."

Daniel pulled a seat out for her beside him. After she sat, she looked around the table at the sea of smiling faces staring back at her. Wendy folded her perfectly manicured hands together on the table. "I hope you had a restful afternoon."

Restful? Definitely not. Melody thought back to her encounter with Guy and how his kiss had ignited a fire in her she hadn't known existed. "It was wonderful."

"Good, because tomorrow you'll meet the bachelors, and from then on it's bound to be a whirlwind."

A waiter came over and filled Melody's water glass. "Would you like a cocktail, miss?"

She looked around the table at all the little umbrellas, each one a different color, and was about to ask for his recommendation when Wendy answered for her.

"She'll have an iced tea. Nonalcoholic iced tea." The producer dismissed the waiter by turning her attention back to Melody. "Can't have you drinking tonight. We need you in top form tomorrow; then after that you may drink whatever you like. In fact, we hope you'll partake in a few cocktails with the bachelors. It'll help to loosen everyone up."

A blush stole up Melody's face. And how loose did they want her? The show aired in prime time, when parents watched with their children. Besides, no matter how many cocktails they had her drink, she would never do anything to compromise her high moral values.

Thankfully, the waiter arrived with her iced tea. She took a long sip, letting the cool liquid slide down her throat. She was nervous enough without now having to worry about the producers wanting her to get intimate with the bachelors.

As if sensing her uneasiness, Daniel reached over and patted her hand. "Melody, you won't have much time to get to know the bachelor's before the first elimination ceremony, so to help you get a feel for them, I brought you their photos. On the back, you'll find some background info." He took a file folder out of the eel-skin briefcase he had propped open on the floor and handed it to her.

"Thank you." She placed it on her lap just as the waiter served dinner.

Although the food looked delicious, she had very little appetite. After eating less than half of her fish and a few bites of her vegetable, Melody set her fork down. All she wanted was to go back to her *bure* and relax.

"You should go to bed, sweetie. You look beat. Besides, I'll be over early in the morning to make you look gorgeous."

Melody nodded, thankful for Sugar's intuitiveness. She slipped the file folder under her arm and bid everyone good night.

A short while later, dressed in her nightgown and slippers, she lay on the rattan sofa, going through the eight-by-ten color glossies of the bachelors. Each one looked better than the last. When she came to Guy's photo, she immediately flipped it over to read his bio and nearly choked. Guy was a count and heir to a tiny kingdom in western Moldavia. She'd been kissed by royalty! Ann and the girls were sure to get a kick out of that.

With her eyes closed, Melody envisioned herself wearing a beautiful brocade ball gown and being swept across the floor by the dashing count. But instead of moving gracefully, her steps a perfect match to his, she stumbled and stepped on his toes. Her eyelids flew open. What kind of daydream was that? She sighed and dropped the picture on the sofa. Guess she wasn't cut out to be a countess.

߀ࠃ

As Guystof unpacked his suitcase, he wondered if he'd made a mistake coming to Fiji. There was no denying Melody had enjoyed his kiss, but that didn't guarantee he'd win her heart. She might be just as attracted to the other bachelors.

He glanced at his roommate, a tall, good-looking fellow with glossy brown hair and gleaming white teeth and wondered if he'd be more to her liking. Then again, as he watched Tommy Spardo primp in front of the large bamboo-framed wall mirror, he doubted she'd fall for the pretty-boy type.

"Hey, Guy, should I gel it or not?" Tommy had his comb poised in midair.

"It's fine the way it is." Guystof folded the last of the shirts Blakesley had packed for him and placed it in the dresser drawer along with the others.

Tommy smoothed back a stray hair before setting down the comb. He studied his reflection a second longer, then headed toward the door. "Wanna join me over at the Island Sun for a couple shots of tequila?"

Guystof wasn't much of a drinker. He liked to keep his wits about him at all times. A vampire never knew when an assassin might be on the hunt for him, although on this island he appeared as mortal as the next bachelor and should be safe from such a threat. Besides, he might learn a thing or two about these men after they had a few too many drinks. "I'll join you there shortly."

He waited until Tommy closed the door and his footsteps disappeared before he slipped the small glass vial from his ring. He put one drop on the tip of his tongue and hoped it would put an end to the ache in his stomach. Due to his jetlag, he'd lost track of when he was supposed to take his next dose. This seemed as good a time as any. And what he didn't need was for his fangs to show.

He smoothed a wrinkle from his shirt, pulled down the crotch of his jeans, and left the *bure*. When he reached the tavern, raucous laughter poured out from inside. He opened the door and was immediately hit with the smell of cigarettes and stale liquor. The haze of smoke made his eyes water, and he wondered if coming here had been such a good idea after all.

From across the long bar, Tommy waved him over, making it impossible for him to leave now. Guystof passed a group of thickly muscled athletes bragging about their sports records as he made his way through the crowd.

Tommy was sitting with two men. One appeared totally disinterested in the bar scene and offered Guystof his seat. The other man had wavy chestnut hair, vivid green eyes, and a physique women must find hard to resist. This bachelor could be stiff competition. Guystof only hoped the man's brains didn't match his brawn.

"Hey, Guy, glad you made it." Tommy slapped him on the back. "This here's Johnny Evans, a philosophy professor at Berkeley," he said, making the introduction.

So much for having a low IQ. "Guy LeBreque, Romanian count. It's a pleasure to meet you." He shook Johnny's outstretched hand firmly, not missing either his or Tommy's shocked expressions.

"You…you're a count?" Tommy sputtered.

"It's not a title I earned, but it's been in my family for generations."

"Well, shit! Like I have a chance in hell with the Dream Girl now. I'm up against a freakin' brain and an aristocrat." The bartender set a beer in front of each of them, and Tommy guzzled half of his immediately. "Oh, well, what I don't have in smarts and breeding, I more than make up for in manners." He let out a loud burp.

The professor looked at Tommy with disgust. "You better watch that crude behavior around the Dream Girl or you might find yourself eliminated."

Tommy laughed and raised his bottle for a toast. "May she have a great sense of humor."

"And be as intelligent as she is beautiful," Johnny added before taking a drink.

She was that and more. Guystof smiled as he remembered the feel of her soft lips on his. Would this afternoon's kiss give him the edge he hoped for? There was no doubt this competition was going to be fierce.

Guystof took one last sip of beer, leaving half the bottle, then pushed it across the bar. "Well, gentlemen, I bid you good night."

"Aw, come on, have another drink. It's on me," Tommy begged.

"Another time." As Guystof left the tavern, he was glad that Tommy had stayed behind. He needed some time alone to prepare for tomorrow. Applying self-tanner was a much bigger job than he'd anticipated.

CHAPTER FOUR

M elody slipped a white tank top over her head, then tied around her waist the red-and-white flower-print sarong Serenie had instructed her to wear. The knock at her door told her Sugar was here to do her hair and makeup as promised. She just hoped the extravagant hair stylist didn't go overboard. Melody preferred simplicity.

She left the bedroom and opened the door to find Sugar struggling with three silver train cases. Melody relieved her of one and set it on a side table in the sitting room.

"Mornin', sweetie. How're you feeling today? You look nervous as hell. Don't worry, when I'm through, you'll feel like a million bucks." Sugar laughed at her pun. "Oops, you're worth that and a whole lot more." She plopped her cases on the table, then pointed at a large overstuffed chair. "Sit."

Melody heeded the order and felt like a specimen in a science experiment with Sugar as the mad professor. The hairstylist draped a black cloth cape around Melody's shoulders, then applied a pink, green, and yellow concealer to her skin. Next she blended a foundation on a plastic artist's palette and applied a dab to Melody's jaw line to check the shade before sponging it over the rest of her face. Not used to wearing so much makeup she was surprised that instead of feeling like a mask, the foundation was light as air.

Sugar carefully applied the rest of Melody's makeup as carefully as a painter creating a masterpiece, then ran a flat iron over her hair, applied a shine polish to the ends and grabbed a mirror from a train case, holding it in front of Melody for her inspection. "Viola! Now you are ready to meet the man of your dreams."

Melody sucked in a deep breath and cautiously peeked at her reflection. "Oh, my! Sugar, you're amazing." She'd been transformed into a princess. And not a gaudy one. Her complexion was radiant, her eyes luminous, and her hair hung in sleek strands of gold down her back.

"Told ya." Sugar's chest puffed out like a proud parent's. "Now go have the time of your life."

"Thank you so much." Melody hugged her close.

"Careful, or you'll muss yourself," she scolded.

Melody left Sugar packing her tools of the trade and wound down the dirt path that led to the beach. She met Wendy along the way.

"Wow! You look incredible." The producer fell in step beside her.

Melody's face heated, and she smiled. "Thank you. I owe it to Sugar."

Before long, they spotted the aqua water sluicing against the shore and twenty stunning bachelors standing before it. All dressed in tropical shirts and khaki pants, they fit right in with the lush island scenery.

She wanted to pinch herself to make sure she wasn't dreaming. These gorgeous men couldn't be waiting for her, little Miss Nobody from Hope. But they were. And each one wished to win her heart.

As she walked closer, she spotted Henry Lyons speaking with the camera crew. Her heart raced and her breath hitched in her throat. She'd forgotten about the cameras! Suddenly, feeling faint, she swayed.

"Easy now," Wendy whispered in her ear as she held her up. "It's okay. Just put one foot in front of the other and keep walking."

Melody didn't know if it was Wendy's calming voice or her fear of making a complete fool of herself that kept her going, but the blood rushed back into her face and her steps grew steadier.

She went to stand beside Henry, who said, not wasting any time, "We're all ready if you are."

Melody nodded and from the corner of her eye saw the cameras begin to roll. She clasped her hands together to quell their trembling.

"The moment we've been waiting for, folks, is finally here," Henry said in his best announcer's voice. "Your new Dream Girl, Melody Johnson."

She pasted a smile upon her lips and focused her gaze on the bachelors. But it was Guy LeBreque's magnetic blue eyes that held her. She recalled his kiss, and for a second, she forgot there were nineteen other men staring at her.

The sound of Henry's voice brought her back to reality. "And our first bachelor is Mark Ritter from Wilmington, Delaware."

Bachelor number one stepped forward and shook her hand. "Nice to meet you, Melody." He smelled of Old Spice—her father's favorite cologne—and the scent made him appear too old for her.

"Bachelor number two," Henry continued, "hails from California. Johnny Evans."

A strikingly handsome man took Melody's hands in his own, causing her pulse to thrum.

"You look beautiful," he said in a soft, sexy voice.

This one was a keeper! She barely heard Henry announce the

rest of the men, Johnny had made such an impression on her. It wasn't until Guy's hand encircled her waist and his mouth brushed the side of her cheek that she came back down to earth.

He raised an ebony brow at her, as if he'd known she was in a fog, and whispered in her ear. "It's wonderful to see you, Melody." His breath tickled her neck, and spikes of electricity shot through her. "Again."

Her cheeks grew hot. She hoped her blush wasn't visible to the camera. "Nice to meet you too," she grumbled, shaking free of his grasp. Guy was going to be trouble. He was much too overconfident for his own good.

The rest of the men were introduced; then Henry announced the five bachelors who'd be going on the first group date. Melody was pleased when she heard Johnny's name called and a bit apprehensive at Guy's, but her excitement returned when she learned she was going snorkeling at the local reefs.

Snorkeling was something she'd always dreamed of doing, but she never imagined she'd actually be given the opportunity to experience it, especially with a group of handsome men.

Perhaps it had worked out for the best that Johnny and Guy had been selected. She was attracted to them both, even if Guy did make her a bit edgy. Having the two bachelors together for the first date would give her the perfect opportunity to get to know them and compare their personalities.

After all, the reason she was there was to pretend to find her soul mate. And she couldn't think of a better way to start things off than to spend the day out on the ocean with those two hot guys.

With a positive attitude, she headed to her *bure* to change her clothes, then meet the men back at the beach for an afternoon adventure.

ജോൽ

It wasn't long after Guystof had dressed that the *lali* drum sounded, calling a meeting at the beach for the group date with Melody. When he arrived there, he spotted the professor leaning up against a tree talking with the other bachelors. Guystof was glad that Johnny was in the group, so that he could keep an eye on the man he believed to be his stiffest competition.

A few minutes later, Melody arrived and the men fell silent. In a pair of cut-offs that hugged her shapely hips to perfection and a low cut tee that did little to conceal her perfectly shaped breasts, it was no wonder the golden-haired goddess knocked the breath out of them.

"Hello, gentlemen. Are you ready to explore the sea with me?" she asked.

The group let out a resounding whoop and followed her through the sand to where a large motorboat awaited them. Guystof hung back from the group and watched Melody climb aboard with the professor right behind, listening raptly to her every word. Guystof boarded last, content to stay in the background, at least for now. When the opportunity was right, he would make his move. Right now, he was content to just enjoy the lovely day.

He leaned against the boat's rail and tipped his head back to let the sun's rays warm his face. He'd never imagined it would feel so glorious, making all the years he'd roamed the dark even more terrible. How could Theo enjoy spending centuries in the cold?

"Where are you?" The sound of Melody's soft voice roused him and he raised a brow at her question.

"You looked worlds away. Were you thinking of Moldavia, Count? Are you homesick?"

Her referring to him by his title sounded odd and much too formal for the casual setting of this tropical island.

"Homesick? No. But I was thinking back over my life, and I can tell you it was not near as pleasant as this… As being here in paradise with you."

The rosy color that flooded her cheeks was endearing. Wasn't she used to compliments or having a man flirt with her? He moved closer so he stood only inches from her. "How would you like to become a countess?"

She stepped back. "That's a little premature, wouldn't you say?"

"Perhaps. But I know what I want when I see it, and I'll do whatever it takes to get it."

"Is that what I am? A prize?" She planted her hands on her hips, the corners of her mouth turned down, and stared at him. "I realized coming into this that some of the men might view this as a game, but the producers assured me all the bachelors here are looking to find love and hopefully a wife."

Guystof smiled. "Oh, rest assured, my dear. I most definitely am looking to find my bride. And I couldn't have envisioned a more beautiful one than you, Melody."

"You're too smooth for your own good." She left him to join the other bachelors who were reclining on lounge chairs at the back of the boat.

Guystof chuckled to himself as he watched her walk away in a huff. Oh, she liked him all right, even if she didn't yet know it.

Melody removed her shorts and tee shirt, revealing her model perfect body in a skimpy silver bikini. The men stared, slack-jawed and a spike of jealousy surged through Guystof, surprising him with its intensity. He was here to win her over, not to develop feelings for her himself.

She donned her goggles and snorkel and jumped off the little platform at the back of the boat. The professor and two other bachelors joined her in the water. Melody seemed to be enjoying herself, especially when a school of colorful, tropical fish swam by her. She put her face in the water and floated on her stomach, a few feet from where Guystof stood on deck watching. Her silver suit reflected the water like tin foil, and he was tempted to ask if she'd remembered her sunscreen, but thought better of it.

A fin broke the surface of the water and headed her way.

Guystof's heart thundered against his chest and a cold sweat broke out along his forehead. "Shark! Melody, swim."

The professor and two other bachelors, farther from the predator and closer to the back of the boat, swam wildly for the stairs. Melody, though, just treaded water and stared, her eyes wide with fear.

"Quick! Give me your hand." He hung over the side of the motorboat, stretching out to her as far as he could. Still she didn't move. And the shark rapidly approached.

"Look at me," he yelled. Her eyes shifted from the shark to his face, and his gaze locked with hers. "Listen to me. Reach out and give me your hand. I promise I won't let anything happen to you. But you have to do as I ask. Now!"

Maybe it was his tone of voice or the way he'd pleaded with her to listen that caused her to break from her shock and reach out to him. Guystof grabbed her wrist, and with every ounce of strength he possessed, hoisted her up. Just as her feet dangled over the side of the boat, the shark swam past and disappeared under the water.

He pulled her close against him, wrapping his arms around her trembling body. "You're safe now," he whispered against her wet hair. Water dripped from everywhere and pooled around his feet.

She clung to him as if he was still her lifeline. "You saved me. I don't know how to thank you."

He could think of any number of ways, but now was not the time to mention them. He inhaled deeply to savor this closeness with her. And smelled blood. To his horror, his mouth began to water and his fangs cut through his gums.

How could this be happening? He'd taken the potion first thing this morning. Blakesley had told him to take it only once a day. Yet, it appeared to be not enough, for he was becoming a monster.

With her neck just inches from him, he could almost taste her sweetness. He moved his mouth along the velvet skin of her throat. His pulse throbbed in his temple, and his desire to sink his teeth into her flesh was almost too much to bear. Oh, why was this happening? He wasn't supposed to have these urgings. Not when he appeared human. And why in hell did he smell blood?

A growl started deep in his belly and threatened to escape his mouth. He gritted his teeth and pressed his lips firmly shut, then took Melody by the elbows and held her out at arms' length. Blood trickled from a cut on her shoulder.

He swallowed hard, the saliva building up in his throat. This couldn't be happening. Not now. Not here. He sensed they had an audience, and from the corner of his eye, he spotted the other bachelors along with the boat's captain staring at him and Melody.

The crowd's noise and the sound of her voice jarred him back to reason. "Guy? What's wrong? You look awful."

He kept his mouth clamped shut and waited for his fangs to recede, before speaking, then focused his gaze on her injured shoulder. "You're hurt."

She looked at her cut. "Oh, that's nothing. I must have gotten it while climbing into the boat. Could have been a whole lot worse." Her cornflower-blue eyes sparkled with gratitude.

"I guess the sight of blood made me realize just how close a call that really was," Guystof said, trying to make an excuse for his bizarre behavior.

"Well, thanks to you, I'm okay." She leaned over and kissed his cheek with lips warm and petal soft.

A burning desire to take her back in his arms raged through him.

Before he could make a move, though, the professor came over and clapped him on the back.

"Hey, hero. Guess what? That shark was a dolphin." A round of laughter and applause followed Johnny's announcement.

Guystof's back stiffened as he watched a playful dolphin trail their boat. When his gaze shifted back to Melody, her face had turned a vivid scarlet. It seemed he wasn't the only one humiliated.

"I guess I'd better go clean this cut up and put some dry clothes on. With that kind of scare, I don't think I'll be going back in the water anytime soon." She glowered at him and walked away.

෨෬

Melody held tight to the railing as she went below deck. The dim lighting of the cabin was a sharp contract to the bright sunshine and it took a minute for her eyes to adjust. She sank onto a sofa and buried her face in her hands.

She'd never been so frightened in her life. Just thinking she might have been eaten by a shark sent prickles of fear up her spine. And it hadn't even been true. What a fool she was! She'd known Guy was melodramatic and would do anything to gain her attention, but she'd never imagined he'd stoop so low as to scare her with a phony shark attack. Yet, he seemed as shocked as she when Johnny pointed out the dolphin. Maybe he hadn't been acting... Oh, she was so confused. She didn't know what to think. But she knew she didn't belong here. She wasn't sophisticated, or worldly, or even brave. She was a meek little mouse who belonged back home in Hope.

A gentle touch to the top of her head startled her, and then she was enveloped in a comforting embrace. She buried her face against Guy's chest. A mix of emotions ran through her. Should she be angry or grateful? If he'd made an honest mistake...

Oh Lord, she did want to give him the benefit of the doubt. Could she be falling for him? But she barely knew him? And he was a

61

count. He could have any woman he wanted. Why her? Could it be that he just wanted to win the game?

He held her closer, her eyes squeezed shut against his strong, muscular chest, then he tilted her chin up and pressed his mouth to hers. Melody's eyes opened wide in horror. This kiss was different. Much different from the one she'd shared with Guy on the beach. And there was good reason for that. The man who held her was not Guy but Johnny Evans.

She pressed her hands firmly against him and tried to push him away but was no match for his strength. His kiss deepened despite her protests. And to make matters worse, Guy stood poised at the top of the stairs. She wanted to cry out to him, "It's not what you think," but by the time she disentangled herself from Johnny, it was too late. Guy was gone.

"What do you think you're doing?" she cried.

Johnny wore a confused look. "Consoling you? You seemed upset."

"I'd call it a little more than consoling." What was it with these men? Why did they think they could kiss her whenever they pleased? Hadn't they ever heard of asking first?

"I'm sorry, Mel."

"—ody. My name is Melody." She grabbed a cushion from the arm of the sofa and hugged it against her chest.

"I was just trying to help, that's all. I guess I got carried away. You're a very attractive woman, Melody."

Johnny looked like a sad puppy that she'd just kicked to the curb. But she didn't care. What concerned her was the image Guy must have of her. After attempting to save her life, not to mention being embarrassed in front of the other bachelors, he finds her locked in another man's arms. Lord, what must he think of her? But what made her even more angry is why she cared so darn much what he thought. If she wanted to kiss every bachelor here, it was her business and no one else's.

She offered Johnny a weak smile. "I shouldn't have snapped at you. I'm sorry. I guess I'm just hormonal."

He squeezed her hand. "Sure. I understand."

Melody watched Johnny leave the cabin. He was the kind of man she should be interested in. She had a lot more in common with a professor than she had with a count. Yet, her heart didn't flutter when Johnny kissed her the way it did with Guy. Men! She was better off without them. *Just let me get through Dream Girl, and then I can go home.*

℠

Theo stared into the large silver goblet. Inside, the image of Melody's lovely face faded into the thick red blood. He'd watched the events unfold in Fiji as a wizard would through his crystal ball and was pleased with what he'd seen.

His brother's humiliation after rescuing Melody from a dolphin had Theo dancing for joy. And then to have Guystof find Melody in the professor's arms was brilliant. Theo couldn't have devised a better plan himself. If that didn't knock his brother down a peg or two, he didn't know what would.

He twirled around the room, his black cape billowing like wings. Theo stopped long enough to drink the entire contents of the goblet, wipe the blood from his mouth with his hand, then lick his fingers. It wouldn't be long until Dragesa was his. He would rule the kingdom as never before. His father and his before that had been weak. They'd listened to their wives, taking care to spare a woman whenever possible. Well, he cared for women too. Cared that they heeded his desires. There wasn't a city or town across the globe that didn't hold a vampire or two that belonged to him. Soon, he could bring them all here, to Dragesa, so that they could service him whenever he pleased.

The thought of those lovely, slender necks his for the piercing, made him quiver with desire.

He'd keep a close watch on Melody. There was no way he was going to lose this battle. Theo slammed the goblet on the thick wooden table and didn't hear the door open behind him. It wasn't until Blakesley was beside him that he noticed the butler. The old man had been with the LeBreques for centuries but mainly served Guystof.

"How many times have I told you not to sneak up on me like that?" Theo snapped.

"I'm sorry, sir. I did knock. And as I'm not light footed to be sure, I felt certain you'd hear me approach."

"Well, I did not. Now what do you want?"

"Your father asked me to call upon you, sir. Shall you be dining with him tonight?"

Theo's gaze settled on the goblet, the side rimmed with blood. "No, tell him I've already eaten."

Blakesley followed his gaze. "Will that be enough, sir? I must say it appears to be no more than an appetizer. There's plenty of meat in the banquet hall. The animals were just freshly slaughtered."

Theo bit back his harsh words. The old man was just doing his job. Or was he? Theo narrowed his eyes and studied Blakesley intently. Perhaps he was spying for Guystof. If that were true, Blakesley would be sorry indeed.

He smiled wickedly. "Thank you, but I'm fine for now. And if I get hungry, I can find someone to satisfy me." Blakesley hated to be fed upon, but if he continued to bother Theo, he would not hesitate to teach him a lesson.

"Yes, sir. Thank you, sir." The old man backed out of the room, not taking his eyes off Theo. It seemed his threat had not gone unnoticed.

After Blakesley closed the door, Theo let out a roar of laughter. He would not be coming around anytime soon.

CHAPTER FIVE

Guystof lay in bed, on top of the sheets, wearing only his boxers. The air was thick and humid. A lone candle on the bedside table gave off the only light. The flame flickered and danced over the wall like a ghost. What was he doing wrong? He'd been so sure Melody liked him. He'd felt the connection when he'd kissed her and again when he held her after pulling her from the water. She'd trembled not just out of fear, but from desire too. Yet, not more than ten minutes later, she was in the professor's arms. The very man who'd embarrassed them in front of the other bachelors.

Not only did Guystof feel like a fool, but he felt betrayed. Although why he should care whom Melody kissed, he couldn't quite figure. Melody was simply a means to an end. He needed a rich wife. She fit the bill. Hadn't he learned from his father the mistakes of the heart? Twice married, both times for love, and both ended tragically. Well, that would not happen to him.

Guystof closed his eyes and was drifting off to sleep when he heard a knock on his door. Had Melody come to apologize? Well, he would give her a piece of his mind, then kiss her like she'd never been kissed before. If that didn't make her forget the professor,

Guystof wasn't the contender he thought he was.

He rose slowly. Let her wait. Better to appear nonchalant than too eager. He started to put on his jeans but kicked them off. He glanced down at his white boxers and smiled. Melody's shock when he greeted her in his underwear would be payback.

Casually, he strolled over to the door with an "Oh, it's you" look pasted on his face. To his surprise, though, the dark-skinned beauty whose family owned the island stood before him. In her arms she held a stack of terry-cloth towels that she nearly dumped at his feet.

"The towels you ordered, Mr. Guy." Her lips, full and red like overripe strawberries, quivered. Her face, warmed by embarrassment, turned a deep rose.

He'd called for towels earlier and had completely forgotten, as his thoughts were focused on Melody and the professor. "Thank you, Serenie."

She gazed at the floor, making a noticeable point not to look at him. "Where would you like these, sir?"

"The dresser is fine." He stepped aside so that she could enter his *bure* and watched her cross the room. "I didn't mean to embarrass you. I thought Tommy had forgotten his key," he fibbed, "or I would have dressed more appropriately."

She giggled. The sound was musical, just like her voice. "That's all right, Mr. Guy. I won't look. Much."

Now it was his turn to laugh. "I'm surprised at you, married lady, to have snuck a peek at all."

She placed the towels in the top drawer of the rattan dresser. "Oh, I'm no longer married. My Joe was killed last year in a fishing accident."

"I'm sorry, Serenie."

"Thank you, Mr. Guy. We had many good years together and three wonderful children. I'm content with my memories."

"You're a fine woman."

She turned to face him, the corners of her mouth turned up in a smile, her stare locked on his, still careful not to look at his physique. "You, sir, are a gentleman." And with that she bowed and left.

He watched her gracefully walk toward the beach, the soft cloth of her sarong hugging her hips, and he couldn't help but admire her. She was indeed a lovely woman. If it weren't for Melody and the fact that he *was* a gentleman...

Tommy entered his line of vision just as Serenie disappeared into the night. Guystof's roommate had been in the last group date with Melody and had gone on a sunset cruise. "How was it?"

Tommy looked down at Guystof's underwear, then out to the beach where he'd just passed Serenie. "Nice. The sunset was spectacular. You wouldn't believe the colors. Man, there's nothing like that back in Oklahoma. But I'd wager a bet you had a better time tonight."

Guystof clapped him on the shoulder. "Do all country boys have such dirty minds?"

"Hell, if I was dressed only in my boxers and alone with a woman like Serenie—"

"Spare me the details." Guystof cut him off. "I know what you would do. But I'm here for Melody. Did you spend much time with her?"

"Yeah, the whole two hours."

Guystof's brows shot up.

Tommy chuckled. "Now don't go gettin' all jealous on me. I know how you tried to save her from a dolphin and all."

Did everyone know about that mishap? "Don't mistake my interest for jealousy. Melody is a grown woman. She can kiss every one of the bachelors, for all I care."

"Kiss? She didn't lock lips with any of the guys on the cruise.

Why, none of us even got any alone time." Tommy shot Guystof an envious look. "Hey, don't tell me you kissed her already."

Guystof wasn't about to tell Tommy about the meeting on the beach that first day. "She kissed the professor."

Tommy sat down on a chair and kicked off his shoes. "Aw, no way. The professor? Can't see Melody with him. I thought for sure, you'd be more to her likin'."

One would think so. "There's no accounting for taste, my friend."

"I hear you. She was so quiet tonight. Almost like she was somewhere else. Maybe wishin' she was back in the professor's arms."

Guystof scowled. "We'll know soon enough who Melody prefers. At tomorrow's elimination." The air in the *bure* had become suffocating. He stepped into his jeans, put on a cotton shirt, and headed toward the door.

"Shit, man! I didn't mean to upset you." Regret tinged Tommy's usually friendly voice.

"I know. And you didn't. I just feel like a walk on the beach." Before leaving the hut, he turned and smiled at the man he knew he could call a friend.

ℂℂ

The wind coming off the water hit Guystof in the face like a wake-up call. He needed to do something and fast, if he was going to make it through and not be sent packing tomorrow. There could be any number of men Melody might choose over him. The professor was a given, but after the whole dolphin/shark fiasco, he had no way of knowing what Melody thought of him or how many other men she might have made a connection with. Damn, this plan to win her heart. The game was a risk, to be sure, but he never imagined how difficult it would be. Sure, women had pursued him over the centuries, but he'd never had to compete with nineteen other men before.

Waves lapped at his ankles, wetting the hem of his pants, as he walked along the beach. The full moon cast a silvery light over the dark ocean. Up ahead the outline of a woman caught his attention. She walked slowly, kicking at the water with her toes. Her sleek dark hair hung down her back, nearly to her waist. Serenie.

A woman's company was just what Guystof needed, and he jogged up to her, careful not to startle her. "Hello, again."

Her eyes opened wide in surprise. "Mr. Guy. What are you doing here?"

"It's a beautiful night. I couldn't sleep, so I went for a walk."

"Most nights are like this. Remember, we are in paradise."

"Yes, and it's a shame to enjoy the stars alone."

She stopped walking and studied his face. "I sense your loneliness, and it makes me sad for you."

Lonely. How perceptive of her. He'd been alone for centuries. By choice. How could it be any other way? He was a monster who had to kill to survive. Of course he was lonely. And would remain so. Even if he did manage to win this game and make Melody his bride, it would not be for love. Besides, once they were married and she discovered what he was and what she would become, she would hate him. And rightly so.

They walked in silence. The wind made conversation difficult. That was all right, though. The night was splendid, and it wasn't very often that Guystof was out in it and not hunting.

He gazed at the men's *bures,* now just tiny dots on the horizon. By now, most of the bachelors would be asleep, making sure to get enough rest so they'd be in top shape for tomorrow's elimination. They would each be given a short time alone with Melody for one last chance to persuade her to keep them around.

Guystof had no idea what he would say to her. His anger and humiliation had not diminished any. He looked over at Serenie, so open and honest, and wished Melody could be more like her, but he was discovering the Dream Girl was a complex woman. And difficult to read.

Up ahead, a row of rocks blocked their path. The giant boulders formed a causeway across the beach and stretched into the sea. On the other side lay Dolphin Bay. Melody's private retreat. He took hold of Serenie's hand and was about to step onto a rock when something moved at the end of the rock pier. He squinted to get a better look. Blonde hair blew in the wind. Melody. Her long white nightgown wiped around her ankles. The gauzy material clung to her, outlining her lithe body perfectly.

Guystof sucked in his breath. She was more beautiful than ever as she stood under the moon and stars. Although she was too far away for him to see her eyes, there was no doubt her gaze was locked on him. She stood there a few seconds longer, then raced down the pier, jumped off the rocks and disappeared into the night.

Serenie looked up at him, and her bottom lip quivered. "Oh, Mr. Guy. Was that Miss Melody on the rocks?"

"Yes. I believe it was."

"Do you think she saw us?" A shadow of alarm touched her face.

"I'm almost certain she did." He tried to keep his tone flat so Serenie wouldn't know that his concern matched hers.

"What if Miss Melody got the wrong impression?" Her big brown eyes were filled with worry. "You're supposed to be here for her, Mr. Guy, not walking along the beach with another woman, even if it was just an innocent stroll. This might have ruined the game for you. Miss Melody might send you home now."

She was right. Melody could very well decide he wasn't the

bachelor for her. But hell, he'd taken a chance just by coming here. No matter what he did, it was a gamble. Hopefully, being seen with Serenie wouldn't end the game for him. And if he was lucky, this might even have played right into his hand. Instead of aggressively pursuing Melody, he'd shift his tactic. Let her come after him. If she was the woman he thought she was, she'd see him as a challenge. One she had to win.

"Don't worry about me. I'll be fine." He kissed Serenie's forehead softly, then slipped his arm around hers. "Come. I'll walk you home."

ℴ&#x3;ℛ

Melody ran through the sand, her toes cut from the rocks that she'd hurried off of, but she didn't feel the pain. What she felt were sharp jabs to her chest. She was a fool! She'd worried all evening about Guy. During her group date, instead of getting to know the other bachelors better, she'd been wondering what Guy was doing. Well, she should have saved herself the heartache. While she'd been agonizing, he was romancing another woman. She should have known what he was. All the signs were there. He was a player! Big time! Yet, a part of her had been starting to fall for his charm.

She'd gone out to the rocks to clear her head. Today had been so confusing. She'd been through a wide range of emotions: fear, hurt, anger, and now this…jealousy. Was that what she was feeling?

Melody stopped running. She turned around and stared at the rocks. What if Guy went out with Serenie to get even? After all, he had seen her kissing the professor.

The cool night wind blew, and she shivered. What she needed was a hot shower to warm her cold body and sleep to clear her muddled head. She had no idea what she was going to do tomorrow. It was the first elimination. Which men should she send home? She knew one thing. She wasn't going to find the answer tonight.

As she approached her *bure,* a dark figure emerged from behind a banana tree. She stopped short. While squinting, she tried to make out the man blocking her door.

"Mel… About earlier today. That kiss. I couldn't stop thinking about it. About you." The professor stepped toward her. His gaze devoured her from head to toe.

The flimsy nightgown she wore made Melody extremely self-conscious. She backed up and held out her hand to ward him off. "Please, Johnny, I'm in no mood to discuss anything that happened today. I'm exhausted. The only thing I want right now is to go to sleep." Her tone was stern, leaving no room for negotiation. "I'll see you tomorrow. Good night!"

She stepped around him to enter her *bure,* closing the door firmly behind her. Good Lord! These men were more than she could handle. How many more days before she could go home?

When Melody woke the next morning, she was no closer than she had been last night at deciding who to eliminate. It wasn't until she stood on the golden sand with twenty men before her, each with his eyes trained on her, hoping and waiting for her to call his name and drape a lei over his head, that she couldn't procrastinate much longer.

Her gaze swept Guy, and, by his rigid stature, she had no idea if he was still interested in her or wanted to be sent home. Perhaps that would be best. They came from two different worlds. She'd never fit into his, and he'd be bored with hers. Wasn't it better to end things now before either, or both, of them got hurt?

Thank goodness she had one more opportunity to talk with the men. Each one had three minutes to impress upon her why he should stay in the game. She hesitated, then called Guy's name.

He came forward, and they walked over to the chairs set in the shade of the trees lining the beach. His icy blue eyes were even frostier than usual, and he made it a point to avoid her gaze. Great. When he should have been trying to win her over, he was doing his best to ignore her. She couldn't for the life of her figure him out.

Best to get right to the point. She sat beside him, and tried to forget that his aftershave was intoxicating. "About last night…"

He leaned back in his chair and crossed his arms over his chest but said nothing.

Okay. So he wasn't going to make this easy. He wasn't going to willingly come forward with why he'd been out with Serenie when he was supposed to only have eyes for her. "On the rocks… I saw you."

"I know," he said flatly.

She sighed. "Look, we don't have much time. I have to make a decision on who stays and who goes."

"And?"

"And!" Her voice rose in pitch and she made a mental note to not let him get under her skin. "If you're not interested in me, please just say so," she hissed under her breath.

"Melody." The way he said her name, like a caress, made her want to slap him. "Should I not be the one to ask you that?"

She ran her hand over her forehead. Had he been with Serenie to get even with her? "Guy, I'm sor—"

Before she could apologize for the incident with the professor, another bachelor, a professional football player she had next to nothing in common with, approached them within hearing range. His huge muscles glistened unnaturally in the hot sun, leaving no doubt that he'd oiled his skin, as if his athleticism wasn't apparent enough without the grease.

"Looks like our time is up." Guy stood.

She smiled, hoping to lighten the mood, but he didn't respond in turn. "I've really enjoyed getting to know you."

The look Guy shot her was more than cold. If she didn't know better she'd have called it deadly. He must really be angry about yesterday.

"Don't kid yourself, Melody, that the brief time you've known me has given you any insight into my life. You know nothing about me."

Her brows rose in surprise. She watched him walk away, his back straight and proud, and in that instant there was no mistaking him for royalty.

"Wow! What got him so pissed off?" The football player plopped into the chair. "You tell him he was going home?" He let out a loud cackle. "Geez, Mel, I promise, if my time's up, I'll leave with a smile on my face. I've had a great time."

Good. Because there wasn't a chance he'd be here tomorrow. She'd barely spoken to him. It was evident he was more into the other bachelors than he was her. One down. How many to go?

After she'd spoken with each man, the brief meetings had done a lot more good than she ever imagined they would. There were quite a few bachelors she could let go without any qualms. She had no interest in them whatsoever. The professor had surprised her, however. After that humiliating day yesterday and that kiss, she'd been almost certain he was a goner. But he'd been truly sorry that he'd caused her any embarrassment and showed her a compassionate side she found quite endearing. Besides, she was here to find a man the public would believe was her soul mate. The man who would become her husband. And the professor fit the bill to a tee. The professor and the wannabe librarian. A perfect match. Then why did her heart thrum for Guy?

There was no denying she was physically attracted to him, but there was more than that to this feeling—this annoying burning sensation that plagued her night and day. He was a puzzle, and by golly, she was going to solve it.

She joined the bachelors back at the water's edge. It was time to make her selections. On a table beside her lay ten fresh-flower leis. She closed her eyes, prayed she'd do the right thing, then called the first name. "Johnny."

When the professor came forward, she thought she saw Guy wince, but she couldn't be sure since he was avoiding her gaze.

Melody looped a lei over Johnny's head. He thanked her and kissed her cheek. The next two names she called seemed to come out of her mouth of their own accord. The men's faces were blurs, and her daze intensified as she realized the next name she called would be the last man to receive an individual date with her. After that, the other six men would go on a group one. Her palms perspired and her knees were weak. She felt as if the air was being sucked from her lungs. *Do the right thing. Please do the right thing.*

"Guy." The relief she felt after saying his name was immeasurable, but her panic returned when he stood before her, unsmiling, his eyes cold and hard. Oh Lord. He wasn't going to accept the lei. He was going to turn her down. She could care less that she was about to be rejected in front of thirty million viewers, but she couldn't bear to think she'd never see him again. She scanned his face, her eyes imploring him to give her the chance to explain so that she could tell him the professor's kiss meant nothing to her.

When he bowed his head, ripples of glee shot through her. She slipped the lei over his head. There was no kiss. Only a brief "thank you" before he turned on his heels and joined the other bachelors back in line. That was okay, though. He was still here and that was all that mattered. She could make it up to him later when they were alone.

Melody selected the next six bachelors; then Henry came forward and asked the ten eliminated men to say a quick good-bye before they had to leave the island.

The bachelors shook hands; then one by one they came over to Melody. The men were very polite, and she didn't sense any heartfelt regrets to be leaving the show. She hadn't made a connection with any of these men, so she felt sure they were anxious to get home and get on with their lives.

Once they departed, it was time for her to select the order of her individual dates. There was no question that she wanted to spend some alone time with Guy. And the sooner the better. So it was a no-brainer when she gave him the first date. After the other selections were made, Henry asked Melody to draw a paper from a basket, then he announced that she and Guy would be visiting a traditional Fijian village and their date would begin now.

Daniel yelled, "Cut," and left his director's chair to pull Melody aside. "This is your first alone date. We need it to be dramatic and emotional. Remember, this isn't real life. Things have to move along quickly. Be sure to show us how you feel about this bachelor."

Before she could answer, Daniel had left her and was back in his chair. "Okay, everybody, places," he announced.

When Melody was in position beside Guy, shooting resumed. Henry led them down a path, where an all-terrain vehicle waited with its engine idling. Guystof offered Melody a hand getting into the truck, then climbed in beside her.

The driver, a small native man, turned from the front and smiled at them. "*Bula!* My name is Solomon, and I'm your guide today."

Before either Melody or Guy could return Solomon's hello, the driver stepped on the gas and the truck sped along the dirt road, nearly tossing Melody into Guy's lap.

"Sorry," she said, clinging tightly to the handrail above her head as they jostled over the rough terrain.

"No need to apologize." Guy draped his arm across her shoulders and flashed her a dazzling smile.

Her heart lurched. The ice between them seemed to have melted, and she knew she was in for a fabulous day. Melody sat back and enjoyed the pristine scenery. Off to the right lay the rainforest. In amongst the thick vegetation, beautiful bright tropical flowers bloomed.

"About yesterday…" Melody shifted her gaze to Guy. "What you saw with the professor, it's not what you think."

Guy lifted a brow at her. "And what is it exactly that you think I'm thinking?"

Melody tensed under his grasp. He was playing games with her. He knew exactly what she meant. Was his ego too big to admit she'd hurt him? "Never mind. I only wanted you to know I didn't kiss Johnny. Just like I didn't kiss you." She turned her head and redirected her gaze out the window.

Guy chuckled and squeezed her arm. "But did you respond to him as you did to me?"

Melody glared at him, then simmered when she saw the sparkle lighting his clear blue eyes. "I don't like it much when a man comes on too strong, even if I find that man very attractive."

"I never would have thought the professor to be your type, but then again, I don't know you well enough to wager a bet on that. I suppose only time will tell who's right for you."

Melody straightened her back. "I'm not the only one allowed to make decisions around here. The men have a say in this game. You have a say." She looked directly into his eyes. "I hope anyone who doesn't feel I could be the one for him would be honest and not accept a lei if I offered it."

"That would be the honorable thing to do," Guystof agreed.

"Would you?"

"What?" he asked, knowing perfectly well what she meant.

"Turn down the lei if you felt we weren't compatible," she

spouted quickly.

"And just what do you think constitutes compatibility, Melody?"

A frown wrinkled her brow. "That's an odd question. Whether a man and a woman get along. Whether they have things in common."

Guystof held her gaze. "Is that so important? Having things in common? Isn't enjoying each other's company more important?"

"Well, yes that matters too. But having the same interests—"

"People can develop similar interests," he said, cutting off her words. "But the spark, the passion has to be there right from the start. And that's what really matters. Don't you agree?"

Melody's face grew warm as she thought back to their meeting on the beach and how his touch, his kiss made her feel as electric as if standing out in a thunderstorm. "Yes." Her voice was low, barely audible.

He reached over and cupped her chin in his hand, tilting it up. "What did you say?"

She swallowed hard. "Yes. Sexual attraction needs to be there."

He leaned in toward her, his mouth just inches from hers. She could see flecks of gold in his eyes she'd never seen before. "Is it"—his lips brushed hers—"there between us?"

This is exactly what Daniel wanted, but her face grew hot with embarrassment that this intimate moment was being filmed for the world to see. Before she could answer, however, Guy's kiss deepened, and against her will, she found herself drowning in his caresses. She wrapped her arms around his neck and held him close so that she could hear the rapid beating of his heart. So much for the cameras and her earlier protests against aggressive men. This one could be forward with her anytime he wanted. With the tip of his tongue, he gently probed her lips apart, and she gladly welcomed him in. His kiss took her where she'd never ventured before. And this body—her body—was responding in unfamiliar ways. But instead of feeling betrayed, she relished the new giddy feeling. Lord, what this man did to her! If this was how she reacted to a simple kiss, what else might be in store for her? My, my, to think that this was what she'd been missing all these long, lonely years.

It took Melody a moment to realize the truck had stopped. Solomon was looking out the window, trying not to appear self-conscious. When she cleared her throat, he slowly turned around.

"We're here," he said. "I didn't want to disturb you while you were busy."

"Oh, um, sorry," she mumbled, running her fingers through her tousled hair.

"Ah, to be young again." Solomon jumped down from his seat while Guy came around and opened her door.

They were in the midst of a small village with *bures* encircling them. People emerged from their huts, dressed in native costume.

An elderly man with a crop of tightly curled gray hair came forward and bowed. "*Ni Sa Bula*," he said.

"*Ni Sa Bula*." Melody and Guy spoke in unison.

"I'm Kari, and I welcome you to my home." He held his hand out, pointing to the *bure* on the left.

"Thank you, Kari. I'm Melody, and this is Guy."

The old man nodded and led the way toward his hut. Solomon bid them good-bye and climbed back into the truck, telling them he'd be back later in the day to take them back to Malaku.

It was cool inside Kari's home. His family sat on the floor around a large wooden bowl filled with a muddy-colored liquid. Melody knew from studying the travelogues that the drink she was looking at must be *yaqona*, the national beverage. The drink was prepared from the pulverized root of the kava plant and a member of the pepper family. She imagined the drink probably needed some getting used to.

Kari motioned for them to sit and an elderly woman, most probably his wife, patted the ground beside her. Melody and Guy sat.

The old woman drank from half a coconut shell then refilled it. "*E dua na bilo*—try a cup?" She passed it to Melody.

The act of sharing a bowl of grog created an invisible bond between the participants, and it would be considered extremely rude not to do so. Melody accepted the coconut but hesitated before putting it to her mouth.

Guy leaned closer and spoke softly so only she could hear. "If it's any consolation, I'm a bit nervous, as well. One swallow and you're done."

Melody gathered her courage and drank. Her tongue tingled and then went numb. The taste, though not unpleasant, was one she hoped to avoid again anytime soon. "Your turn," she whispered, refilling the coconut. As she handed it over to Guy, a fuzzy-headedness took hold, and she swayed.

"I wouldn't plan on standing anytime soon or I may have to catch you when you fall."

"I wouldn't mind. I like being in your arms." Through her foggy euphoria, she realized what she'd just said. Wow! That grog really packed a punch. She'd better be careful, or who knew what might come out of her mouth next.

Guy swallowed the *yaqona* quickly, giving no indication of like or dislike for the drink. Outside the hut, someone played the guitar. Its hauntingly sweet melody increased the calming effect the kava was having on Melody. She leaned against Guy and he wrapped his arm around her waist.

She closed her eyes and relaxed, breathing in the masculine, sexy scent of his cologne and finding it perfectly intoxicating. Or maybe she was just intoxicated. Either way, she was in heaven.

"Do you think it would be rude if we went outside?" he asked.

Melody looked up into his smiling face and instantly knew what he meant. Spending time alone with him was exactly what she wanted too. "I don't think they'd mind."

He stood first and it was a good thing, because when Melody got to her feet, it felt as if the ground moved beneath her.

Guy helped to steady her by placing his strong arms around her. "Whoa. I think you're going to need some assistance."

She nodded, thanked Kari and his family for their hospitality, and left the hut with Guy holding her up. She wondered why the grog seemed to have no effect on him, then brushed it off on account of how much bigger he was than she.

They strolled down a dirt path with the camera crew following behind. Soon they came upon a lagoon, and although Melody would have loved to get closer to it, the sides were ringed with mud flats and thick vegetation. Guy took hold of her hand and led her to a grassy spot where they could relax by the lake and get to know one another better. He sat first, and then pulled her down beside him. He sprawled his long, muscular legs out in front of him, then turned on his side to face her, leaning on his elbow and resting his chin in his hand. With ice-blue eyes, he stared at her as if he wanted to look deep into her soul.

"I don't envy you your position here. All the men vying for your attention, and you have to try to figure out who's sincere and who's not."

Melody blinked in surprise. That seemed an odd thing for him to say. She knew there might be bachelors who had other motives for being on the show besides finding true love, but she hadn't been focusing on that and to have it brought up by Guy made her wonder if he might not be referring to himself. Her heart lurched. She prayed that wasn't the case. "I suppose some of the bachelors might be here for the fame. Though I hadn't spent much time worrying about that.

But since you brought it up, what are your reasons for being here?"

Guy chuckled softly. She loved the sound of his laugh. It was deep and throaty and extremely sexy. "You need to ask me that? Didn't I tell you the first time we met that you were going to be my wife? That was no joke, Melody."

His gaze penetrated right down to her toes, and she tingled all over. "How could you have meant that? You didn't even know me."

He lifted one ebony brow slightly. "Ah, but I knew of you. I knew you weren't a frivolous person, that you have high moral values. You love your family and friends and the fortune that you won has been bringing you more problems than happiness."

Melody gasped. "You knew all that about me? How?"

He sucked on a blade of grass before answering. "Some I learned from the newspapers, but the rest I learned from watching you on the beach. A first impression can tell a lot about a person."

Hmmm. That was true. Her first impression of him had been mixed. Though she'd found him extremely attractive, he also was aware of his allure and he used it to his advantage. That kind of self-assurance she was unfamiliar with and not quite sure she liked. So, if her first impression had been one she'd stuck with Guy might have been eliminated from the game already. Thank goodness, she didn't put much stock in them.

"How did you know the money had been a problem?" she asked.

He rolled onto his back and looked up at the sky. The sun highlighted his high cheekbones and square jaw. Gosh, he was handsome.

"A woman like you," he said, almost as if speaking to the wind, "beautiful, intelligent, kind, should be able to have any man she wants, but when you add a fortune to that combination a problem occurs. How does she know if the man that she wants is in love with her or her money? Men no doubt would have come out of the woodwork to meet you. Am I correct?"

She sighed. The memory of the headaches she and her friends ensued because of the endless stream of gold-digging men was still very fresh. "Yes."

"And that, my dear, is why you are here."

"So you think you know me?"

He smiled, exposing his white teeth. "Not nearly as well as I'd like to."

Pat answer, she thought, though she did like it. "And what more would you like to know?" She lay down beside him, but instead of watching the clouds pass by, she watched him.

He shifted his gaze back to her. "What are you looking for in a man, Melody?"

Although that was not an unusual question, she thought hard about it. There were many qualities she'd look for in her future mate, but one stood out above the others. "Honesty. Without that, a relationship has nothing. And how can one expect to build a life with someone if it's based on lies?"

"I agree." But his gaze dropped, and she thought she sensed him withdraw from her.

Could he be hiding something? Maybe there was more to his wanting a wife than he let on. But then as if reading her mind, he moved closer to her and picking up a strand of her hair, rolled it between his fingers.

"Since we're talking about honesty, would you be willing to leave your loved ones behind and move across the world?" he asked. "After all, Romania is a long way from New York."

He'd caught her off guard. She didn't know how to answer that question. She'd never considered leaving Hope before. She'd always assumed that was where she'd stay. Maybe because she'd just never had a real reason to leave before. But faced with having to choose between her hometown and the man she loved, well, that was a difficult decision, indeed.

"I-I don't know." She chewed her bottom lip and thought best how to explain her feelings to him. "I really don't think I can answer you. I mean, I suppose if I were really, truly in love and that man asked me to marry him, I think then, yes, I would move to the ends of the earth for him. I think. But I really can't say for sure, unless I was actually in that situation." Oh Lord. She must have sounded like a fool.

"Thank you. You were honest, and I appreciate that too."

She studied his fabulous eyes. They were filled with tenderness and passion. He reached for her, and she went eagerly into his arms. Gently, he brushed her hair back from her forehead, and the feel of his hand on her skin sent spasms of desire through her. She wanted him to touch her, caress her in places that couldn't be shown on TV. If only they weren't being filmed...

Melody lifted a shaky hand and stroked the side of his face. She was surprised by its softness. No rough stubble scratched her fingertips. She ran her lips along his throat, tasting his skin. When her mouth covered his, he pulled her closer, their kiss deepening. She closed her eyes, losing herself in desire.

"Ah, Melody, you are so lovely," he murmured against her ear, then kissed her again with such intensity that she was left dizzy.

Waves of passion rolled over her. Their chemistry was insane. Daniel and the producers would be thrilled, but if she didn't stop now, this PG-rated show might become too hot for family viewing.

She ended their kiss, then said, "I've had a wonderful time, but it's getting late. We should go."

He glanced briefly at the camera crew and whispered so that only she could hear, "We'll pick up where we left off later."

CHAPTER SIX

As Guystof helped Melody to her feet, his stomach rumbled and a nauseating feeling took hold. This problem was happening more often and he kept taking more of the potion. Yet, it didn't alleviate the sickness, at least not altogether. Taking hold of Melody's hand, he walked with her back to the village. Solomon stood by the truck. He waved at them, and they hurried over to the vehicle.

"I hope you haven't been waiting long?" Melody asked.

"Not to worry, Miss Melody. Once I take you back, I go home to wife and ten children." He winked at her. "So no hurry."

Guystof and Melody climbed into the truck. Once they were seated, she placed her small hand in his and he squeezed gently. They rode back in silence, but it was a comfortable silence. He was more at ease in her company now, feeling he had secured his position in the game until the very end. There was no doubt in his mind that he'd receive a lei at the elimination ceremony tomorrow night. She had more dates to go on but he wasn't worried. Guystof had developed a bond with Melody that the other bachelors would be hard-pressed to break.

Back at Malaku, he kissed her good-bye. It was a sweet kiss void of the passion they'd shared earlier, but just as nice. "Thank you. I had a wonderful day. I hope you did as well."

"It couldn't have been better. And there's no one I'd have rather spent it with." Melody smiled, then turned and walked in the direction of her *bure*.

Guystof would have liked to watch her disappear from view, gleaning great pleasure out of the graceful sway of her shapely hips, but his nausea urged him to hurry back to his hut. Once inside, he slipped off his ring and removed the tiny vial. Only half remained! He placed a drop on his tongue, then set the vial on the dresser while he awaited relief, hoping he could make due with just that one drop. So much for Blakesley's prescription. His dosage amount had worked for only the first day.

He sank into an overstuffed chair and put his feet upon the footstool. An instant later the squeak of the door indicated Tommy had arrived.

With a towel wrapped around his waist and a bottle of sunscreen in his hand, Guystof's roommate flopped down on the bed. "Shit! That sun is strong. I was at the pool less than an hour and I feel like a french fry." He glanced down at his arm glowing red and beginning to blister, then up at Guystof. "Hey, how was your date?"

"Nice."

Tommy chuckled. "You spent the entire day with the Dream Girl and all you have to say is 'nice.' Don't tell me you two didn't click. Is there something wrong with her? Something I should know? Or maybe she didn't connect with you. Maybe she's into someone else. Maybe she has a thing for me." His laughter continued while Guystof stared at him. "I'm sorry. I'm not laughing at you. The sun must have gotten to me, fried my brain along with the rest of me. Or maybe this competition is too much for me. I like Melody. Really, I do. She seems like a great gal. But I'm not used to sharing a woman with lots of other men. I mean, what do you think she's doing on those dates? You don't suppose she's…"

Guystof scowled. Did the buffoon really think Melody was that kind of woman?

Tommy must have noticed the look on his face, because all traces of laughter disappeared. "Oh, shit, man. I didn't mean to imply you did anything with her. I can tell you're a gentleman and all. You're royalty. Don't you guys follow all kinds of fancy protocol? I'll bet you don't even kiss a girl until after you've had a dozen dates."

Now it was Guystof's turn to laugh. Tommy was unlike any mortal he'd ever known. "You really are an ignorant fool."

Tommy broke into ripples of laughter again. "I'm so glad you've got a good sense of humor, man, 'cause I'd hate to have to defend myself against you. Never dueled before."

I wouldn't need a sword or a pistol to end your life. One bite would do the trick. "Care to join me for dinner?"

"Sure. Just have to shower first." He walked over to the closet and rifled through his clothes, then looked over his shoulder at Guystof. "I don't have a clean shirt. I put my laundry outside the door this morning like we're supposed to. Got my pants back, but no shirts." He puffed out his chest and pummeled it with his fists like Tarzan. "Do you think I could dine half nude?"

Guystof shook his head. The corners of his mouth twitched as he tried to keep from smiling.

"Well then, I guess I'll have to borrow one from you," Tommy said.

Guystof pointed to the top drawer of the dresser and watched as his roommate danced across the room, letting the towel drop from around his hips to expose his neon swimsuit.

Tommy fingered through the pile of shirts, pulling out a pale yellow one. He held it up against his chest to study his reflection in the mirror, but the corner hem caught the vial of potion, knocking it onto the floor.

Guystof leapt to his feet. Shock and horror raged through him. His stomach tightened into a knot, and excessive saliva formed in his mouth. It's not Tommy's fault. It's not his fault, he reminded himself as the tips of his fangs broke through his gum line. It was an accident. He squeezed his hands into fists, not caring that his nails cut into his palms. *Fight! Fight! Fight the rage. You're not a monster. You're as close to human as you'll ever be. And you don't have to react this way. Killing isn't the answer. It won't provide more potion.*

It would have been easy to sink his teeth into the side of the man's neck, making him pay for his actions with his life, but Guystof summoned all his control and swallowed hard, forcing the fangs to recede. He hadn't noticed Tommy's back pinned to the dresser or the look of panic plastered over his face.

"Shit! I'm sorry, Guy." His eyes looked like two chocolate cookies—big and round and dark. "Was that medicine? Do you have more?"

Guystof shook his head.

"I'll bet if we asked Henry…or the producers…they could find a doctor to get you some more. Right? What was that stuff, anyway?" Tommy's nostril's flared as a sour odor wafted up from the floor.

"No doctors, no producers. You're not to say a word. Got it?" Guystof's tone was harsh, and he immediately regretted having spoken to Tommy that way when he saw the guilt-ridden expression on his friend's face. "I'll be fine, don't worry." He picked up the vial, relieved that it hadn't broken, but having no way of knowing how much he'd lost on the floor.

Tommy escaped to the bathroom, but paused outside the door. "Don't tell me, Guy. Are you taking Viagra?"

He had no idea what Tommy was referring to, but, wishing more than anything that his roommate would take his shower and leave him alone, he nodded.

"Lordy, Lordy, your secret's safe with me," Tommy said before closing the door.

Guystof leaned back on his heels and placed his head in his hands. He hoped he could make the potion last or the game would soon be over for him. He envisioned his life the way it used to be, and a cold sweat broke out over his forehead. He would become a vampire—a full-fledged monster—and all that entailed. His thirst for blood would return, and without the criminals he'd found so readily available on the streets of London, he'd have to target innocent people here on Fiji—people he'd come to know and like. He'd become like his brother, and that was a fate worse than death.

ⅎℛ

Melody couldn't stop thinking about the count. He wasn't the snobbish aristocrat she'd thought him to be. He was thoughtful and kind. And when he touched her, she felt as if she was on fire. He ignited a flame in her that she hadn't known existed. And his kisses made her sizzle, leaving her hungering for more. She'd never felt like that with a man before, not even Greg Sinclair. And she'd been so sure she was in love with him. Well, if she'd thought that was love, then what in the world was this?

Fear tightened her chest. What if Guy's feelings for her weren't as strong as the ones she had for him? She couldn't get hurt again. This time it would be even more painful...because she was a woman now. A woman who was falling in love.

She slipped the sleeveless pink dress she'd been holding over her head and let it fall softly over her body; then she stared at her reflection in the mirror.

Her eyes, usually a blue somewhere between the ocean and the sky, now glistened like sapphires. Her complexion, though always clear and milky, had never been this radiant. Oh boy! She was headed for trouble. Big trouble. She wasn't falling in love. She was already there. It was as if Guy had waved a magic wand and cast his spell on her.

"What should I do?" she asked her reflection, as if this new and different young woman would have the answer the old Melody couldn't find. But as expected, her reflection merely stared back blankly at her, no words bubbled forth from between her freshly kissed lips. This was a problem she would have to solve and no amount of magic was going to do it for her.

As she continued to dress for her date with the professor, she couldn't help but wish that it was Guy she'd be dining with. She closed her eyes and envisioned him ordering dinner for her, then feeding her chunks of fresh pineapple with his fork. But the smile that curved her lips soon turned to a frown when she realized how unfair she was being to the other bachelors, and guilt washed over her.

She had weeks to go yet as the Dream Girl, and here she was acting as if the game was over. She'd selected her bachelor and they would soon head off to his fairy-tale kingdom where they would live happily ever after. Well, this was no dream and she knew from experience that dreams didn't come true. She needed a reality check and fast. A lot could happen before the end of the game. For all she knew, her feelings for Guy could do an about face. He just might turn out to be the self-centered count she'd thought him to be from the start.

Holding on to that thought, she touched up Sugar's perfect makeup application from this morning with a gold shimmer lip gloss, picked up her black sequin handbag and marched out the door convinced she would have a wonderful time with Johnny Evans.

An hour later, she sat across from the bachelor at an intimate corner table in one of the island's best restaurants, awaiting dinner. The flickering orange flames from the votive candles in the centerpiece cast shadows over his face, elongating it and giving him an unnatural, almost sinister appearance. Ridiculous, she knew. The professor was a sweet, soft-spoken man, and just the sort of man she should have been attracted to—had been initially, if not for Guy.

But despite her best efforts, she couldn't stop thinking about the count and comparing him to the man across from her. Strong, self-assured, and used to getting what he wanted, Guy was the complete opposite of this reserved philosophy teacher.

"What are you thinking?" Johnny reached across the table and placed his hand over hers. Her first reaction was to pull back and hide her hands under the table, but that would have been rude. And the last thing she wanted to do was hurt this man's feelings. He'd been nothing but polite to her—a perfect gentleman. Again the comparison popped into her head and a slight smile curved her lips. Guy was many things, but a perfect gentleman? She wasn't so sure about that. And thank goodness, she thought with a devilish grin, imagining the feel of his strong hands on her body.

"Hello, Melody." Johnny patted her hands. "I wish you would let me in on what you find so amusing. I'm afraid you're having a better time with your thoughts than you are with me."

She directed her attention back to the professor but was at a complete loss for words. What in heaven's name could she say? Thankfully, the waiter arrived with their food, temporarily shifting the attention away from her and onto the meal.

She glanced at her plate—smoked marlin in a creamy basil white sauce served over pasta, then over to Johnny's pan-fired oyster kebabs. She hoped he hadn't ordered that dish for its aphrodisiac affects. Her worry increased when he refilled their glasses with Chardonnay and drank most of his before taking the first bite of his meal.

Remember, he's a gentleman, she reminded herself as she cut a piece of fish and popped it in her mouth. She continued to eat, hoping he would do the same, thus eliminating the need for conversation. But to her dismay he refilled his glass and stared at her over the rim.

"You look exceptionally beautiful tonight. Quite ravished."

She chewed quickly to keep from choking.

"—ing. I mean ravishing." Johnny took a long sip, then set his glass down and picked up his fork. The tip of his nose had turned beet red.

Oh, no. The man couldn't be tipsy, could he? He'd only had two glasses of wine. But then she had no way of knowing what he might have consumed before their date. Great. Her quiet professor might turn out to be a drunk.

"Thank you." She smiled sweetly but continued to eat without making any attempt at conversation.

Johnny must have gotten her message, because he did the same, alternating between bites of oyster and sips of white wine.

When the waiter returned to clear their plates he asked each of them in his thick Indian accent—more than half the population of Fiji was Indian—if they'd like a cup of kava. No, no, no, she wanted to scream. No kava. She definitely did not need the fuzzy-headed feeling she'd gotten when she drank the *yaqona* with Guy.

Melody had the uncanny feeling she was going to need all her wits about her if she was going to make it home without any mishaps from her date with the professor.

℠∓℞

Theo flung the goblet he used as a crystal ball against the wall, spraying blood across the room. Damn that Johnny Evans. And damn that brother of his. At the rate things were going, the professor would be eliminated from the game by tomorrow night, leaving Guystof well on his way to a wedding ring on his finger and a new bride on his arm.

Well, there was no way he was going to allow that to happen. He'd rot in hell first. Theo strode across the room. With his forefinger, he stopped a smear of blood from dripping onto the floor, then licked his fingertip, savoring every drop. His lips quivered and his fangs emerged. But he would not give in to his hunger now. It would have to wait. There were more important matters to care for…like dealing with that senseless professor.

He crossed his arms over his chest, placing his hands on his shoulders, squeezed his eyes shut and visualized Fiji. When he opened his eyes, he was at the beach, the turquoise water lapping over his feet and the pale moonlight glinting over his head. Ah, magic was such a wonderful thing!

A southwest breeze blew his hair across his face. He raked it back, then headed in the direction of Johnny Evan's *bure*. He found the professor easily, asleep in his bed. The drunken fool. Johnny wouldn't be a challenge at all. Using his magic again, Theo transformed himself into a fly. He buzzed around the bachelor's head a few times before landing on his upper lip. When Johnny twitched, Theo flew inside his mouth and took control of the professor's soul.

CHAPTER SEVEN

Melody had spent the last week smiling and making pleasant conversation with men she had no interest in, while the man she did care about was probably lounging by the pool sipping margaritas. She wondered if Guy was spending as much time thinking about her as she was about him. She leaned back in the chair and let out a sigh.

Sugar pulled on the strand of hair she'd been brushing and yanked Melody's head. "If you don't sit up straight, I'm never gonna finish your hair." Although she tried to sound harsh, Melody knew she meant no offense. Sugar had good reason to hurry. This evening there was another elimination ceremony.

The ten bachelors would soon be cut to five. There was no question the count was staying, but who the other four keepers would be, she still hadn't a clue. Most of the remaining men were on a pretty even playing field. She could easily pick the names out of a basket and be happy with the results. The only one she was uncertain of was the professor. After that dinner fiasco, she wasn't sure she wanted to keep him around. But she supposed she owed him the benefit of the doubt. He might have just been having an off night.

Sugar pulled Melody's hair up into a twist, secured it to the top of her head with some hairpins, then applied her makeup. She finished it off by dusting translucent powder over Melody's face, then stood back and admired the finished product. "You look fabulous as always, hon, but I can tell you're nervous."

Melody patted the woman's hands. She had become so much more than just her hairstylist/makeup artist. Sugar had become her friend. "I'm fine. Just a few butterflies in my stomach, that's all. I have to let some of the men go; and I really hate to hurt their feelings."

"Sooo, is there one who's really caught your eye. A bachelor that might be Mr. Right?"

"You know I can't tell you that. You'll just have to wait and see along with everyone else," Melody scolded.

Sugar set her hands on her hips. "I know that. I didn't want you to tell me his name. Just a simple yes, or no would be fine."

Melody smiled. "Maybe."

"When did you become so cold-hearted? Can't you see the suspense is killing me?"

Melody rolled her eyes at Sugar's melodrama and kissed the side of her cheek. "Thank you once again for making me look beautiful. As soon as the gag order has been lifted, I promise, you'll be the first person I pour my heart out to."

She left the *bure* and headed toward the beach. It was a beautiful night. Hundreds of stars twinkled overhead, helping to light her way. As she neared the sand, instead of finding the bachelors lined up nicely along the water's edge, they stood huddled together with the crew, Daniel Stone, Henry, and the producers.

Wendy waved Melody to join them. She knew something was terribly wrong and hurried over. Despite the night, she could see their faces were pale and grim. Oh Lord. What had happened? She scanned the crowd, wondering if someone had been injured, or worse. To her relief, everyone was accounted for.

"What's wrong?" she asked breathlessly.

All eyes turned to the director.

"I didn't want to alarm anyone, but you all need to know so that you might take the proper precautions," Daniel said.

Melody's heart raced so fast surely it was about to jump right out of her chest. "What's happened?" Her voice sounded unlike her own. Small and very far away.

Daniel drew in a deep breath and let it out slowly before speaking. "I was recently informed by the authorities that the carcasses of numerous sheep and goats were found not far from here."

Melody's stomach lurched. "Oh dear. How awful. Have they found the animal responsible for the killings?"

He shifted his weight, obviously agitated. "I'm afraid they don't think it's an animal that did this."

Melody's eyes widened in fear. "I don't understand."

"Not only was the flesh eaten, but the bodies were drained of blood too."

It took Melody a second to realize the loud gasp had come from her. Her knees grew weak, and before she hit the ground, strong arms encircled her waist and held her steady. She gazed up into Guy's clear blue eyes and immediately felt safer.

"There's no animal known to do that to its prey." Daniel hesitated a second before continuing. "But there were tribes of cannibals that did. They were supposed to have disappeared sometime in the 1800s, though."

"Apparently not."

Melody shifted her gaze to the professor. He stood slightly apart from the rest of the group. Dark rings encircled his red glassy eyes.

He looked as if he either hadn't slept a wink last night or was suffering from a terrible hangover.

Daniel shot Johnny a warning look and said dryly, "It looks like there might be a tribe that exists somewhere on the island. The theory is they must live deep in the rain forest and for some reason have become emboldened enough to venture into civilization."

Guy tightened his hold on Melody, and she cast him an appreciative half smile.

"Security on Malaku has been increased, and I want you all to feel assured that we will do all we can to ensure your safety. There are a few more things I'd like to go over with you before we go forward with the elimination ceremony. If there are any bachelors who, after hearing this news, no longer want to continue with the game, now is the time to come forward. The producers will understand as I'm sure Melody will too."

She looked over the faces of the men she'd come to know and care about. "Of course. No question about it. If I was in your spot, I'm not sure what I would do."

Sam, a family therapist and one of the bachelors she'd barely had any alone time with, stepped forward. "I'm sorry, Melody. Nothing against you. You seem like a wonderful woman, but I'm divorced and have two kids. If I only had to worry about myself, I might stay and get to know you better, see where it might lead, but my kids come first. They need their father. Alive."

Melody slipped out of Guy's arms and shook Sam's hand, then kissed his cheek. "No need to explain. It was a pleasure to have met you."

"Anyone else?" Daniel chimed in.

A short, stocky man with thickly rimmed tortoiseshell glasses came forward. Melody couldn't remember his name. She thought he was a doctor of some sorts and so shy he'd barely said two words to her during his group date. "I should go too. My patients…my practice. Sorry." He pushed his glasses up the bridge of his nose then went to stand beside Sam.

Three more men came forward. Melody scanned the faces of the five remaining bachelors, as did Daniel, wondering if any would remain to the end. The group remained silent.

"Well, then. That makes it easy. No need for an elimination tonight, after all. Oh, and another thing. I spoke with Tristate's insurance carrier, and due to the liability factor, we're going to wrap production ASAP. So, Melody, that means instead of five alone dates, tomorrow afternoon we'll do one group date, you'll select your bachelor, and it's a wrap; then we're off this island." Daniel turned to leave but looked back over his shoulder. "I almost forgot. No one is to go anywhere alone. Understood?"

A resounding "Got it" ensued. Melody said good-bye to the men leaving and was glad they were going to wrap up the shooting early. She hadn't been given a choice to leave and since she wasn't especially brave she would be none too glad to be far, far away from what she had once considered a tropical paradise.

Wendy and Eddie Hatch strolled over to her. "Care to join us for dinner and a drink at the Island Sun?"

Melody's back stiffened at their offer. She couldn't believe they could think about food after hearing Daniel's announcement. Obviously, they had stronger stomachs than she had. "No thanks. I think I'll call it an early night."

Guy appeared alongside her. "You two go on, I'll walk Melody home."

Wendy raised her pencil thin auburn brows and looked to Melody for confirmation.

"That's fine. I'll see you guys tomorrow." Melody watched the producers disappear from view. Tommy and two other bachelors were headed in the same direction, but the professor stood alone in the shadows. When she caught him watching her with a look she couldn't quite decipher, he shifted his gaze away and looked out at the ocean. Despite the still-humid night, for some reason a chill ran over her skin.

"Ready?" Guystof draped his arm casually over her shoulder as if he'd done so many times before.

"Yes." She walked with him along the bronzed beach, forgoing the road. Pleased that he chose the long way to her *bure*, she relaxed against the comfort of his arm and pushed the disturbing thoughts of cannibals from her mind. She was safe with him. Of that she had no doubt.

⁊Ɇ

Guystof gritted his teeth as pain stabbed his insides. His stomach ached as never before. He'd cut back on the potion, hoping to make it last until the end of the show. If Melody found out about the monster trapped inside him, not only would he lose his kingdom to Theo, but she'd look at him with fear and loathing.

"Are you all right?" Melody asked, her sweet voice edged with concern.

"A bit of indigestion. Most likely brought on by Daniel's news. And I'm sure I'm not the only one suffering from it."

Melody stopped walking, sinking her heels into the sand and bringing him to a halt beside her. "Thank you for staying."

His gaze searched her lovely cornflower eyes, trying to determine if she was merely being polite or if she truly was glad. Almost as if reading his mind, she added, "I mean it. You, I especially wanted to stay."

He raised his brows at her. "Really? Even though at times I'm cocky and overbearing?"

"Despite your flaws." She laughed, and he felt her relax against him.

"I might be many things, Melody, but a coward is not one of them. No cannibals are going to keep me away from you." Though he doubted very much that was what was responsible for the killing of the animals. Theo's hand or, more precisely, fangs were all over the incident. The only problem was he hadn't made his presence known, which could mean he might have taken another form. Theo could appear at any time as anyone or anything. Guystof had to keep his guard up at all times.

He wasn't surprised that his brother would travel to Fiji. As the game drew to the end, the more desperate Theo would become. And the more dangerous. For his brother would stop at nothing to keep him from succeeding at father's ultimatum. Well, Guystof was just as determined to win.

"Are you in a rush to get back home," he asked Melody, bringing his mouth close to her ear so his lips brushed the side of her cheek. "We've had so little time alone…together… The night is so lovely." As he spoke the words he looked straight into her eyes.

"What did you have in mind?"

"Sitting here." He pointed to an alcove jutting out from the shore sheltered by groupings of large weather-beaten rocks. "Under the stars getting to know you better."

She did not pause to think it over, nor did she hesitate when she answered. "Sounds lovely."

Guystof smiled and took her small soft hand in his, then led her through the sand. He chose a secluded spot sure to be far from prying eyes and sat. Melody kicked off her sandals and did the same.

She leaned back on her elbows and looked up at the sky. "Let's say—hypothetically, of course—that I chose you. What would you say?"

"Do you mean would I accept your lei? Or would I become your husband?"

"Both."

"Why do you doubt me? Didn't I tell you the very first time I laid eyes on you that you were going to be my wife?"

She dug her toes into the sand. "That was you just being arrogant and flirty. And that's exactly what has me concerned. I'm not sure if this is just a game to you. One—being that I can tell you're highly competitive—you're going to win."

He reached over to her and removed her hairpins one by one, letting her hair stream down her back to reflect the moonlight like spun gold. "What's it going to take to make you believe me? Don't you believe in love at first sight?"

She sucked in her breath, shrugged her shoulders, and stared deep into his eyes. He leaned in toward her and brought his mouth down on hers. Her lips tasted as sweet as he remembered. Then he tasted the buttery soft skin of her throat, and it too was like honey.

He brought his kisses lower, to the tops of her softly rounded breasts where her cleavage showed from the V-neckline of her silk dress. Gently, he pushed open the silky material, exposing to him even more of her beauty. He cupped her breasts in his hands, then kissed each nipple until it turned rosy and hard.

She arched her back, and he wrapped his arms around her waist, pulling her closer to him until the beating of her heart blended with his own and he could no longer tell where one stopped and the other began.

He ran his hands over her hips, pressing her against his thigh, then he slipped his hand under her dress and pushed the material up over her knees. In the faint glow of the moon, he admired her satiny smooth skin. With his fingers he traced circles on her thighs and her legs quivered beneath his touch. He moved his hand up over her taut, flat belly, then slipped it down inside her panties. The area between her legs was moist and warm, and she did not so much as flinch when he touched her there.

This woman, this wonderful woman, seemed willing to accept his lovemaking. Yet, an unfamiliar deep ache stirred in his chest. While he lay aroused and ready to enter her, his heart said no.

Melody trusted him. She believed he was as he appeared, when everything about him was a lie. His mouth went dry. Cold horror froze him. Was this guilt that he felt? Why should he care if he took advantage of her? Soon, he would take her life, plunging her into the black abyss of eternal hell.

He jerked back his hand, then pulled down her dress to cover her nakedness. He couldn't hide from his feelings any longer. He did care. The thought of her looking at him with eyes full of anger and despair when she learned he'd been dishonest with her and had used her as a pawn would be more painful than a stake driven through his heart. No, if he were to have her, she would have to come to him of her own will, knowing the monster that he was and loving him in spite of it. If he must take her mortal life, at least he could leave her with her dignity.

She lay there beside him, unmoving and silent, the only noise the gentle waves lapping against the shore. Her brilliant blue eyes questioned him. "What's wrong?" Her voice was husky with emotion.

He wanted to take her back in his arms and kiss away her fears, but he couldn't do that. "Nothing. It's late. I should take you home." Guystof stood, brushed the sand from his clothes, and held out his hand to help her up.

She slapped it away. Those eyes that had looked lovingly at him only moments ago had changed as quickly as storm clouds blowing in over the sea. "How dare you dismiss me like that, as if I have no say in this? Do you think I take this lightly? I was willing to give myself to you, as I've never done with any man. Do you know how hard that was for me?"

Melody was a virgin! He could hardly believe his good fortune. Imagine spending centuries with a woman who'd never been spoiled by another man. She would belong to him and only him forever. But at this moment, he didn't know what to say. Any response would have to be a lie, for he couldn't tell her the truth. And hadn't he told enough lies already? "I'm sorry. It's not you. It's me." He couldn't stand the pain he saw on her face and the distrust in her eyes, so he turned his back to her and looked out over the sea.

Less than a minute later, she was beside him, her sandals clenched in her hand so that her knuckles had turned red. "Walk me home, or don't. I really don't care." She stormed down the beach where the water met the sand, her feet shooting out little sprays of water with each step she took.

Guystof did not blame her for being angry and hurt. But his compassion may have just cost him the game.

ဆဘ

Melody's emotions were running helter-skelter. She wanted to lash out at Guy for hurting her, and the next instant she wanted to beg him to take her back in his arms. She'd been so sure he wanted her as much as she wanted him. Lord knew she'd never felt like this before. So she'd thrown caution to the wind and look where it had gotten her. A slap in the face and a thank-you-very-much-ma'am, but-no-thank-you, from the man she was falling in love with. How could she have been so wrong? How could she have misread him so?

Guy had been coming on strong from the instant she laid eyes on him when he stepped from the ocean like a Greek god. Telling her she was going to be his wife. Talking about love at first sight. Well, it looked like she was the only one feeling that way. She must have been right all along, thinking he was too good to be true. She was a fool! Why would a handsome count want a naïve small-town girl? Well, he didn't and now she looked like an idiot practically throwing herself at him. She'd waited twenty-four years to make love and she was willing to throw it all away for a wild night of passion on the beach. She should be thankful that he stopped her, for she had to have lost her mind.

Up ahead the lights of her *bure* cut through the dark like a beacon. She was on her private beach now and hurried across the sand. When she reached the path that led to her front door, she turned to Guy. He'd stayed about ten feet behind her, at least having the good sense to keep his distance. "You don't have to come any farther. Good night."

He nodded. "Good night, Melody."

That was it. That's all he had to say. He was going to let her go just like that. "All right then, good night." She raced up the path not knowing whether he watched her enter her *bure* or not. What did it matter? For whatever reason, he must have decided she wasn't the woman for him after all. At least there was one thing about him she'd been wrong about. He was a gentleman! He could very well have taken advantage of her tonight and then dumped her tomorrow. Thankfully, she didn't have to experience that humiliation. She'd be the one doing the dumping. There'd be no lei for Guy at the next elimination ceremony.

Melody slammed the door shut behind her, then pressed her back against it and slid down onto the floor. Tears filled her eyes and she covered her face with her hands.

"Melody."

She started at the sound of her name. Who was there in her *bure*? She fanned her fingers apart and looked between them.

Standing before her, tall and gaunt, his eyes dilated and dark, was the professor.

"What are you doing here? You have no right to be in my *bure*."

She hoped to sound strong and assertive, but inside she trembled like a helpless lamb.

He chuckled softly. "I'm afraid you're wrong about that. For you see, I have every right to be here, because very soon you will belong to me."

He sounded odd, unlike himself. Oh Lord, he must be drunk again. She pushed her back harder against the door and slithered up it so she could reach the knob. But when her fingers curled around it, the deadbolt turned, locking her in. Her eyes widened in fear and her heart thundered against her chest. She tried to turn the latch but it wouldn't budge.

She shifted her gaze to the professor. "H-how did you do that?"

"It's quite simple, my dear. Magic."

Magic? What was happening? "What do you want?"

"Now don't be afraid. I'm not going to hurt you. I'm just making sure that you choose me for the last bachelor."

Ha, fat chance. He was insane if he thought locking her in her hut would ensure him of that.

"Come." He walked over to the bar and poured two glasses of wine, then held one out to her. "Drink with me. I can assure you this wine tastes like no other."

Her mind was awhirl as she tried to think of ways out of this. "If I have a drink with you, then will you leave?"

"Absolutely."

When she took the glass from him, her fingers brushed his, and they were cold as ice.

"Cheers." He drank his quickly, then watched for her to take a sip.

As she lifted the glass to her lips, she was struck by the dark red color and thick consistency of the wine. She took a sip and gagged. Blood! He'd given her blood? The glass slipped from her fingers and crashed to the floor.

"You'll get used to it, my dear. It just takes some time."

She scrunched her face in horror and shrank away from him. "What are you? Some sort of monster?"

"Some think that, but I don't like to. No one's all bad. I must have some redeeming qualities, though I'm hard-pressed to say what they are." He reached out and grabbed her by the shoulders.

"Let go of me," she hissed.

He laughed and tightened his hold, his cold fingers pressing into her skin. "Look into my eyes."

"You're crazy." She tried to turn away, but his glassy stare locked with hers and held her captive. His eyes were lifeless and seemingly pupilless. She opened her mouth to scream but her throat had closed up and no sound would come out. She tried to lift her foot to run, but it was as if it were cemented to the floor. All she could do was stare at his horrid pale face and pray that the power of movement would return to her.

His thin, shrunken lips moved and his voice sounded odd and far away. "You drank wine with me, a wine such as you've never tasted before. A wine that has bonded us. From now on whenever you hear my voice, you will come to me. Do you understand?"

The room seemed to tilt, and his sinister image faded in and out. When she wobbled, he pulled her into his arms. *Nooo*, she wanted to scream, but her lips were stiff and dry.

He whispered in her ear, "I asked you a question, Melody."

She shuddered at the foul smell of his breath. "Yes." The word came forth as if of its own accord.

"Good. Now repeat after me. You shall have no rival."

"You shall have no rival."

"I will only have eyes for you."

"I will only have eyes for you."

"That's my girl." He gave her a brief hug, then blew his stale breath in her ear.

And everything went black.

CHAPTER EIGHT

*G*uystof lay in bed. The pains in his stomach had returned, but they were nothing compared to the pain in his heart. What was happening to him? Not only did he look human, but he was feeling human too. These emotions he felt were like none that he'd ever experienced before, and he didn't know what to do with them.

When he'd first met Melody he'd been attracted to her, and why not? She was a beautiful woman. Besides, marrying someone attractive was far better than spending centuries with someone he found distasteful.

This game should have been easy. All he had to do was get her to fall in love with him. What he never expected, though, was to be the one who fell.

He squeezed his eyes shut, and Melody's lovely heart-shaped face appeared in his mind's eye. How could he have been such a fool? He should have known from the last time he was alone with her that to get too close—to hold her, kiss her, touch her smooth, velvet skin—would mean nothing but trouble. She did things to him that no other woman had ever done. And now he'd blown it. She felt rejected, and he'd probably be the next bachelor asked to leave the island.

His chest tightened. The thought of never seeing her again hurt worse than the thought of losing his legacy. He would have to find a way to make her understand why he hadn't made love to her tonight. And do it without telling her more lies. Guystof switched off the lamp on the bedside table and rolled onto his side. Perhaps a solution would come to him in his sleep.

Unfortunately, the next morning when he awakened, his problem still weighed heavily upon his mind. Today was the last group date and possibly the last opportunity he would have to talk with Melody.

He showered and dressed quickly and was out the door before Tommy had even gotten out of bed. Guystof hoped to beat the other bachelors to the beach and grab some alone time with Melody, but when he arrived, she was engrossed in conversation with the professor.

Melody looked as gorgeous as ever. She wore a bright yellow sundress and matching sandals. Her hair was loose and full, falling softly over her shoulders, just the way Guystof liked it best. She seemed in good spirits, laughing and flirting with Johnny. If this was how she planned her revenge, it was working. Pangs of jealousy already stabbed at Guystof's heart. Deep down he knew she didn't care for the professor, not in the way she cared for him, but that didn't stop him from feeling hurt nonetheless.

Well, he wasn't going to let her see that it bothered him. He walked nonchalantly over to them. "Good morning, Melody, Johnny."

The professor offered a brief hello, while Melody remained silent, never taking her focus off the professor.

Guystof bristled. He understood that she was angry with him, but he hadn't expected her to be rude. He stepped between them, forcing Melody to look at him. Her eyes, lifeless, lusterless orbs, seemed to look right through him.

He took hold of her arm. "Melody, what's wrong with you? I know you're upset with me, but you don't seem yourself."

She remained silent, simply staring past him to where the professor stood. Guystof turned, shifting his gaze to Johnny as well. The professor raised a brow, then smiled smugly. Something was wrong. Horribly so. It wasn't like Johnny to gloat.

Guystof studied him more carefully. The professor looked pale, unusually pale, and his eyes, despite being bloodshot, held a devilish twinkle Guystof had never noticed before. Guystof let go of Melody's arm, and she returned to the professor's side. Whatever was going on between Melody and Johnny, he was going to find out and put a stop to it.

Tommy and the two other bachelors were approaching, along with Henry, Daniel, and the crew. It was a good thing too, because Guystof's temper had started to flare, and he was afraid, if left unattended, he might say or do something he'd later regret, perhaps even pushing Melody further away.

"I'm glad everyone's here," Henry said cheerfully. "Today's the last date, a group date, and you'll all enjoy a wonderful Fijian *Magiti*. The feast will consist of lots of traditional specialties cooked in an underground oven, but best of all, it will be served beside a spectacular tropical waterfall."

Guystof could care less what they ate or where they went. All he cared about was getting Melody alone so he could find out what was going on.

"Follow me," Henry continued. "It's within walking distance."

Tommy and the bachelors fell in step with Henry, Daniel, and the crew, while Melody and the professor lagged behind enough to carry on a private conversation. Guystof took up the rear and kept a close watch over Melody.

When they came to the waterfall, the crew set up the cameras, and within a short time, they were filming the second-to-last episode of *Dream Girl*.

The professor was still monopolizing Melody's time, and she was acting as if he was the only man around. Not only did she ignore Guystof, but she paid no attention to the other bachelors either. Tommy and the other men didn't seem to mind. They must have assumed they had next to no shot of being chosen as the last bachelor and were content just to have a good time.

Guystof tried again to speak with Melody. "About last night. Please, just give me two minutes to explain."

He shouldn't have wasted his breath. She turned to the professor, whispered something in his ear, and the two of them walked hand in hand down to the base of the waterfall. Then, to his astonishment, she removed her sundress, revealing the same hot-pink string bikini she'd worn the day he met her. She dove into the water and beckoned for the professor to join her.

Guystof had been angry before, but it was nothing compared to the way he felt now. If he didn't know better, he'd think the professor had put Melody under some sort of trance. His chest tightened. Could that be it? A trance. He watched as the professor stripped down to his swimsuit, and then, as if he knew Guystof was watching him, he looked over his shoulder and grinned. His eyes twinkled in a devilish way, so unlike the professor yet so familiar to Guystof.

Theo! He should have known his brother was behind this.

He waited until the professor and Melody swam under the waterfall before he headed down the dirt path toward the men's *bures*. He found the professor's quickly.

Guystof tried the door, but it wouldn't budge. He pointed his finger at the lock, hoping his powers still worked. With the way the potion had been making him feel, he wasn't sure about anything. But to his relief, the handle turned and the door swung open, filling the sitting room with bright sunshine. The room was neat, and nothing looked out of the ordinary. He walked toward the bedroom. The shades were all drawn, making the room pitch-dark. He flipped on the wall switch. The recessed ceiling lights came on and illuminated the room.

There were two beds, one noticeably not slept in. The professor's roommate had been eliminated early on. Guystof went over to the bed with the rumpled sheets. He needed to find out who really slept there. If his hunch about the professor was correct, then he was about to discover that Theo was posing as Johnny.

Guystof took off his shirt and ran it over the bed, then held it over his face and looked through his shirtsleeve as if peering into a crystal ball. Theo's handsome face emerged, confirming that he'd been using the professor as his pawn.

A vein pulsed at the side of Guystof's neck. Theo had Melody under a spell.

He slipped his shirt back on and left the professor's *bure*. When he arrived back at the waterfall, he was pleased that no one seemed to have noticed that he'd been gone. Melody and the professor were still in the water, too wrapped up in each other to notice anyone else. The other bachelors were sprawled out on hammocks, lounging in the shade of huge, lush banana trees.

A group of Fijian dancers dressed in colorful costumes waited to perform. Three long wooden tables were grouped together and set up buffet style, while one set apart from the others had place settings and chairs.

Guystof watched as the sizzling, steaming food was removed from the underground oven and placed on the tables. Though not the least bit hungry, he would make an attempt to eat while he hoped to seize upon any opportunity that presented itself to steal Melody away from the professor.

The *lali* drum sounded, indicating dinner. The bachelors joined him at the buffet, but it took Melody and the professor longer to arrive.

Johnny draped a towel over Melody's shoulders and rubbed them dry; then they both slipped their clothes on over their swimsuits and strolled hand in hand over to the group, taking their places in the buffet line.

It took all of Guystof's willpower to keep from racing over to them and socking the professor in the jaw. But that would serve no purpose other than to make Guystof look like he'd lost his mind.

Once everyone had filled their plates and taken their seats, a choir of Fijians began a serenade and the dancers put on a spectacular performance. There was very little chance for conversation, which was just as well since it was useless trying to speak with Melody as long as Theo had her under his control.

It was quite evident Guystof would not have the opportunity during this group date to have any time with Melody, not with the "professor" keeping a close watch over her. He would have to wait until later, when everyone had retired for the night.

৪৩৫

At just before midnight, Guystof tiptoed out of his *bure*, careful not to wake Tommy, and snuck over to Melody's hut. He peered in through her bedroom window, and as he'd hoped, she was asleep.

Quietly, he opened her window and stepped into the room. He crept over to her bed and removed the pillowcase from the spare pillow beside her. Using it as a gag, he bound it tightly over her mouth so she couldn't scream; then he slipped one arm under her head and the other arm under the curve of her back. As he lifted her from the bed, her eyelids flew open. Shock and terror were reflected in her gorgeous eyes and not a speck of recognition. That bastard! Theo must have wiped out any memory of him from her mind.

She struggled in his arms, trying to break free. His hold on her tightened, and he clasped her against his chest, feeling the beat of her heart and the softness of her breast. She was light as a child, and he carried her with ease out of the bedroom and across the sitting room. Pointing his finger at the front door, he used his power to open it and strode into the night, heading for the thick foliage of the rainforest. A full moon helped to light his way.

A tangle of vegetation whipped at his face as he crashed through the jungle, but he barely felt it, so determined was he to remove this terrible spell Theo had placed on Melody and have the woman he loved back. He set her down at the base of a thick mangrove tree.

"Don't try to run," he warned. "This forest is full of creatures you wouldn't care to meet."

Melody's eyes became huge saucers, and she tilted her head up and stared at the branches above her. A choir of frogs sang their night song, and she shuddered.

"Don't be afraid. I'll keep you safe." With his shoe, he drew a magic circle on the ground, then ushered Melody inside. He stepped back and waited for a cloud to partially cover the moon so that a shadow was cast between them.

"An evil creature has caused this trouble to befall us. He holds you captive, and just like the wolf devours sheep, he has turned you into his chattel. His slave. His food."

Melody stared at him, her face pale, her lips just as colorless. Dark purple shadows of worry and fear lined her magnetic blue eyes, now empty and void of memory. She shivered and wrapped her arms across her chest, covering her breasts, nearly visible through her thin white nightgown.

"Release her," Guystof cried into the night, "for she is mine. You have not played fair, brother."

A flash of blue-white lightning lit up the sky and revealed Theo. He stood about ten yards away.

"Did you think your magic so superior to my own that I wouldn't discover you were disguised as the professor?" Guystof asked. "You always underestimate me, brother."

Theo's mouth curled into a snarl. "I suppose I do, though you've never given me reason to do otherwise."

"Release her from your trance or do battle with me. And you will never underestimate me again." Although Theo had an advantage with his magic skills, Guystof was a much better fighter.

Theo hesitated but stepped into the circle with Melody. He removed her gag, then took hold of her hands. "You are no longer under my spell. You no longer belong to me and will have no memory of this when you awaken." His voice was low but loud enough for Guystof to hear.

Theo looked over his shoulder at his brother. "The game is not over yet," he spat, then blew in Melody's ear and disappeared.

She swayed, and Guystof lunged forward just in time to keep her from hitting the ground. He grabbed her by the waist and pulled her into his arms.

"I almost lost you," he murmured against her cheek.

"What happened? I feel like I've been asleep forever." She studied his face. "Why did you say you almost lost me?" Before he could answer, she placed her hands on his chest and pushed back from him. "I remember now. We were on the beach. We were about to… You didn't want me… I should be really angry with you, but right now I don't feel anything but numb."

"That's good."

She raised her finely arched brows at him. "It is?"

"Yes. Numb is much better than angry."

She laughed softly. "I think I must agree."

He bent his head down and pressed his mouth on hers, and he thought this to be the sweetest kiss he'd ever tasted.

When their lips parted, she looked down at her thin nightgown. "What are we doing out in the jungle, and why am I dressed like this?"

"It's the middle of the night, for one thing, and the rest is a very long story," he replied.

"Well, I'd love to hear it, but if you don't mind, I'd prefer doing so back in my *bure*."

"My thoughts exactly." He scooped her into his arms and carried her through the rainforest.

Inside her *bure*, he placed her gently upon the bed, then pulled the covers up over her. "The nights here can be quite chilly, if you're not properly dressed."

"As if I had any say in the matter," she quipped.

"I'd rather you catch a cold than have something worse happen to you." The words came from his heart and rolled off his tongue. What was he to do? He hated the game of deception he'd been playing, and he certainly didn't want to take her mortal life. Yet, that was exactly what he was going to do. If he tricked her into marriage, then he would be no better than his brother.

Pain shot through his stomach, and he bit his lip to stifle the groan that rose up in his throat. Damn the curse that had made him a monster, and damn that potion for burning his insides.

He looked over at Melody, her knees tucked up under her chin, her hair falling in ringlets over her shoulders, and she looked no more than fourteen, an innocent child who had no idea what fate had in store for her.

Guystof strode across the room. "I'm going to make a pot of

tea; then I have some things to tell you."

ℬℭ

Melody watched as Guy left the bedroom. He was a proud man, and she could tell something weighed heavily on his mind. She should still be angry with him for humiliating her yesterday on the beach, but that anger had faded and not returned. Whatever had happened to her today, whatever danger she'd been in, she owed her safety to Guy. Perhaps she'd misjudged him. Maybe he really did care for her and was thinking not of himself but of her. Maybe that was why he'd cut their lovemaking short. Wouldn't a gentleman respect her and not take advantage of the heat of the moment?

She knew the answer to that. And she also knew that Guy was the man she'd always been waiting for. Her soul mate. In a few short hours, she'd choose her bachelor, and there was no doubt in her mind who that would be. Then she could tell Guy exactly how she felt about him and they could plan their future together.

She leaned back against the pillows and closed her eyes. Ann, Mags, and Billy would just die when they discovered she really had found the man of her dreams on a reality show. Her parents would adore him. Oh, she couldn't wait to introduce him to her friends and family.

Melody let out a sigh of pure joy. Who knew becoming the Dream Girl would change her life so completely? She owed Ann in a big way!

Guy returned carrying a rattan tray. On it were two steaming mugs of tea and a bowl of chocolate candy kisses.

She smiled up at him. "How'd you do that so fast? Magic?"

"Hardly. You'd be amazed at how well equipped this *bure* is. If you're hungry, I'll bet I could find us something more substantial."

She shook her head. "This is fine. I'll stick with the kisses, candy or otherwise."

He grinned at her and set the tray on the bedside table. "Well, you're feeling better already, I can see." He handed her a mug. "Careful, it's hot," he warned as she brought it up to her mouth.

She blew into the cup, never shifting her gaze from his handsome face. He sat on the edge of the bed, his demeanor changing. His clear blue eyes darkened and became filled with sorrow. He opened his mouth to speak, then quickly clamped it shut.

Melody set her mug back on the tray and reached for his hand. "What is it? Whatever happened today, I can take it. All that matters is that I'm safe now and here with you."

A hint of a smile curved his sensuous mouth. "Ah, my dear, there is so much you don't know."

"Then tell me. We have all night."

"What I have to tell you goes back hundreds of years."

"Then condense it as much as you can," she said, trying to lighten his mood. "We have the rest of our lives for you to tell me the story."

He stared at her so intensely it was as if he wanted to look straight into her soul. "You are so beautiful, Melody. And not only on the outside. Everything about you is wonderful. I only hope you can forgive me."

Fear gripped her heart like an icy glove. She squeezed his hand. "What, Guy? Please just tell me."

He looked at her a little longer, then stood and walked over to the window, his gaze turned to the night. "There are no cannibals on Fiji."

Joy filled her as she studied his back. "Thank goodness. That's wonderful news." But something inside her told her this happiness would be short-lived.

"Unfortunately, my brother is much worse."

She swung her legs over the side of the bed, placing her feet flat on the floor. "Brother?"

"Yes. You know him."

"I do?" She went to him and pressed her hand to the small of his back, relief flooding through her. "Is that it? Is that what has you so troubled? Is he one of the bachelors?" She thought hard, trying to figure out which one it could be.

He turned to her and swept her into his arms, pressing her against his hard, muscular chest and holding her as if he never wanted to let her go. She wrapped her hands around his neck and covered his mouth with her own. She kissed him with all the passion and love she felt, trying to reassure him that nothing would alter her feelings for him.

He kissed her back with equal desire, then whispered against her hair, "No, love, he is not one of the bachelors. You met him at the airport on your way here."

She thought back over her trip to Fiji, and her brow furrowed; then her back stiffened. "The only person I met—"

"Was the handsome Romanian," Guy answered for her.

She uncurled her arms from his neck so they hung limply at her sides. "But you said you didn't know him. You lied to me?"

He took a deep breath, then let it out slowly. "Yes." He took her chin in his hand and brought her lowered gaze up to meet his own. "Whatever you think of me after tonight, remember one thing, Melody. I love you. And I've never uttered those words to anyone before."

Oh, how she'd wanted to hear those words, but not like this. "I don't care about your brother, and I don't care who your family is. All I care about is you. So if you're about to destroy what we have, don't tell me any more." She covered her ears with her hands.

Gently, he brought her hands back down to her sides. "Dear, sweet Melody. I'm afraid not wanting to know is not going to make this go away."

Her chest tightened. "I don't understand why you're doing this."

"I have no choice. I could never live with myself if I wasn't completely honest with you. Especially knowing how you value honesty above all else." He tightened his arms around her and she buried her face in his shirt.

"I am not who you think I am."

She lifted her head and looked up at him. "If you're not really a count, so what? Actually, I'm relieved. I was having trouble seeing myself as a countess anyway."

He kissed the top of her head. "I'm afraid that's not it. I am a count. But I have no fortune. My home has fallen into ruin. So you see, my motives for coming here were not honorable."

Her mouth went dry, and she swallowed hard the lump that was threatening to choke her. This couldn't be happening. She'd left Hope for a secluded tropical island to get away from the gold-digging men who'd been hounding her, and she'd fallen right into the arms of the biggest offender.

She wriggled free of his hold and backed away from him. "You've been using me for my money?" She wanted to scream at him, but her words came out as little more than a squeak.

"At first." He hung his head. "I was given an ultimatum by my father to find a wealthy bride in sixty days or lose my legacy to my brother. Melody, I had no choice. Theo is horrible. You have no idea what he is capable of."

He lifted his head and his eyes locked with hers. "That was then, before I met you. It has nothing to do with now…the way I feel about you now. I love you. Not your money."

She looked at him skeptically. "Why should I believe you?"

He shrugged. "I have nothing to gain by lying."

Her ears rang and her muscles ached. She felt as if she'd been run over by a truck. She didn't know what to think. "Then why tell me this now? Why confess at all? Unless it was to ease your guilty conscience."

"Because I can't continue this charade any longer."

"What charade? I don't know what you're talking about. Or what this has to do with why I was in the rainforest in the middle of the night dressed only in my nightgown. What did you do to me?"

He walked over to the bed, sank onto it, and held his head in his hands. "Five hundred years ago, a curse was put upon my family. My grandfather tried to develop a potion that would reverse the spell, but he was burned at the stake before he could test it thoroughly. My brother, the evil monster that he is, put you in a trance and tried to steal you away from me."

"Guy, you must know how all that sounds. I mean, come on. A curse, spells, a trance? I don't believe in hocus-pocus."

He raised his head and looked at her. His eyes were dark and tortured. "I know it sounds crazy, but it's the truth."

Obviously, he wasn't going to tell her what really happened. At least not now. What did it matter anyway what his motives had been? He'd saved her from his brother, and if he loved her now, then wasn't that all that mattered? Despite her better judgment, she sat next to him.

"I am a vampire." His voice broke, and a look of tired sadness passed over his features.

"What?" She must have misunderstood him. "Did you say you were a vampire?"

He nodded.

A tumble of confused thoughts and feelings assailed her. "Okay, I know you wouldn't joke at a time like this, so that means you must be delusional. And that also means I've fallen in love with a madman. So, Guy, please, I'm begging you. Tell me the truth."

"I am." He held her gaze with such a burning intensity that she knew he wasn't lying.

It took a second for his words to sink in, and when they did, her skin prickled with fear. "But how can you be a vampire? I've seen you out in the sun. And you eat food. You don't drink blood."

"My grandfather's potion makes me appear human and able to do all the things you do. But if I stop taking it, all my vampire traits will return."

"And what then?" She shrank away from him. "Will you drink my blood?"

His expression darkened. "Believe me, I don't want to."

"But you will. Was your plan to make me a vampire too?" When he didn't answer, the tension stretched ever tighter between them. "Will it be very painful?" Images of long, sharp fangs piercing her neck appeared in her mind.

"That depends. I'll be as gentle as possible."

"What if I say no? Will you go away and let me live my life, or don't I have a say in this?"

He drew in a sharp breath. "I won't force you to do anything."

Her heart squeezed in anguish as the reality of what he was and what he wanted her to become began to sink in. "I want to have children someday and be able to grow old."

"You will. We'll have lots of children. And we'll even grow old together. Vampires age, just very, very slowly."

This was all too much for her to take in right now. "I need time to think. I have to be alone." Her steady voice masked her inner turmoil.

She didn't have to tell him a second time. He rose from the bed, his shoulders hunched, and left the room without looking back. A moment later, she heard the front door open, then shut.

With trembling hands, she covered her face, as a war of

emotions raged within her. A warning voice in her head told her to beware. A life with Guy would bring danger and uncertainty. While her heart told her a life without him would be passionless and empty.

Torn between commonsense and emotion, she left the *bure* and, like a zombie, headed down to the beach. Sand sifted between her bare toes and a broken seashell scraped the bottom of her foot, but she didn't feel the pain. Nor did she feel the rush of cold over her skin as she entered the water. She pushed forward until the water reached the tops of her thighs. Staring out across the sparkling azure water, she watched the dawn break over the horizon and wished for an answer. But it never came. Later, when she returned to her *bure*, she collapsed on the bed and fell asleep, still having no idea what she was going to do.

CHAPTER NINE

"**W**ake up! Wake up!"

Someone was shaking Melody's shoulders and screaming in her ear. It took a while for the fogginess to leave her head, and she cracked an eye to see who had been so rude as to awaken her from her dream. She caught a glimpse of bright copper hair, then focused on Sugar's face. Frown lines creased Sugar's foundation and drooped the corners of her painted red lips.

"You must have had some night last night, girl. I'm one for partyin' and all, but you look awful," Sugar scolded. "I sure hope whatever you did with whoever was worth it."

Memories of last night came flooding back, and she grabbed the blankets at the foot of the bed and pulled them up over her head.

"Oh, no, you don't." Sugar yanked them back. "I don't care if you're still hungover, you're getting up."

"I'm not hungover," Melody moaned.

"Well, hungover or not, you've slept most of the day away and in about an hour you're going to announce to the world the bachelor you've chosen as the man for you. Now come on." Sugar took hold of her arm and pulled her up. "I know I've said many times that I'm an artiste, but I ain't no miracle worker. So get going. I turned the shower on." Sugar pushed her toward the bathroom.

Melody heard the spray of water from the doorway. Although she could care less that they were filming the last episode of *Dream Girl* today, she was freezing, and a hot shower would do a lot toward warming her up. She let the water pummel the back of her neck, relaxing her stress-tightened muscles. Just as she started to feel a bit better, Guy's face would come to mind and she'd be filled with misery again.

She grabbed a bar of coconut soap, lathered up her skin, and watched the suds rinse down the drain. If only she could wash away her memories too.

Just when her tired, cold body had begun to warm, Sugar pounded on the bathroom door. "Hurry it up in there, hon. We've got lots to do."

Melody let the water stream over her head one more time before turning off the shower. She grabbed a large, fluffy towel, dried off, and slipped into her robe; then she took another towel and wrapped it around her head. She padded over to the fogged mirror above the sink and wiped clean a section using her palm. Boy, she was a mess! Dark circles and bags under her eyes, sallow skin… Sugar really did have her work cut out for her today.

When Melody went back in the bedroom, the first thing she noticed was the gorgeous gold sarong laid out for her on the bed.

"You like?" Sugar asked with a hopeful gleam in her eyes. "The producers let me pick it out for you myself. After all, I have come to know your taste, right Mel?"

She was able to muster up a faint smile. "I like it just fine."

Sugar patted an armchair by the window. "Come and sit down and tell me what's got you so sad."

Melody plopped down. With a big sigh, she said, "I don't even know where to begin."

"At the beginning's usually good."

"Do you know why I agreed to be the Dream Girl?"

Sugar shook her head as she removed the towel from Melody's hair. Long strands cascaded down her back, wetting her robe.

"Because I was tired of men only being interested in my money."

"And you thought these men would be different?" Sugar asked, combing through her hair.

"Yes... No... What I mean is, I didn't really care why the men were here. I thought if I pretended to fall in love and staged a phony engagement, everyone would leave me alone."

Sugar lifted a penciled-in brow at her. "So then what's the problem?"

"I never planned on actually falling in love."

"Like I said. What's the problem? Don't he love you?"

Melody sank lower in the chair. "That's not it. I'm pretty sure he does. It's just that he's not at all like what he led me to believe. I mean he's totally different."

Sugar ran the blow dryer over Melody's hair. "Different's not always bad. Different can be good."

"Oh, believe me. In this case, it's very bad."

Sugar clicked off the dryer and came around to stand in front of Melody. "I'm a firm believer in love conquers all. If I loved a guy and he loved me back, I'd do everything I could to make things work out. Sometimes you've just gotta compromise, Mel."

Compromise. How does one compromise with a vampire? She thought about that as Sugar applied her makeup; then she went back over her life. She thought about all those dateless years spent reading her beloved books and dreaming about the wonderful hero's she'd found in those pages. But those men didn't keep her warm at night or bring her chocolate kisses.

She thought about the long, lonely years ahead of her. Someday her friends would marry, and where would that leave her? A spinster. That's where. Love didn't come around often. Lucky for her it happened this once.

Maybe a compromise wasn't such a bad idea. After all, becoming a vampire might not be so awful. She could spend a thousand years with Guy. Melody waited for Sugar to finish applying her mascara, and then she sprang up from the chair and bolted out the door.

"Wait." Sugar chased after her with makeup case in hand. "I still have to apply your lip gloss."

"It'll have to wait," Melody shouted over her shoulder as she raced in the direction of the men's *bures*.

"Where are you going?" Sugar caught up with Melody and sprinted alongside her.

Melody shot her hairdresser a huge grin. "I've decided to take your advice. I'm going to compromise."

₲ѓ

Perspiration rolled down Guystof's neck. His stomach wrenched with pain. He'd taken the last of the potion, but there had barely been enough to wet his tongue. What did it matter anyway? There was no need for him to continue with this charade. No need for him to appear human. Melody knew the truth about him. And despised him. His stint on *Dream Girl* was over. He looked down at the foot of the bed where his bags were packed. As soon as these pains subsided, he would be on his way home. Not only had Theo won, but Guystof had lost the only woman he'd ever loved.

When the door burst open and Melody charged inside, he could barely believe his eyes. Another woman, a makeup artist, if his memory served him, though he barely took notice of her, hovered in the doorway.

Melody came around to the bed, concern etched on her face by the lines on her forehead. "What's wrong? Are you ill?"

Guystof rolled onto his side and brought his knees up to his chest. "Is it that apparent?" he moaned.

"And why are your suitcases packed? We haven't had the final elimination yet." Then, as if it just occurred to her, she leaned over him, her hair brushing his neckline and smelling like coconuts, and said, "You're leaving, aren't you? You weren't coming to the ceremony. You were leaving me." Her eyes blazed with anger.

He bit back a groan. "You shouldn't be here, Melody." He lifted the belt to her bathrobe. "And certainly not dressed like this."

She looked down at the silk print robe as if for the first time she realized what she wore. "That doesn't matter. What I care about is you. What's wrong?"

"That potion I was telling you about. The one my grandfather made… The one I've been taking…to appear human. It's been making me sick. Maybe I haven't been taking enough."

"How much are you supposed to take?"

"I started with one drop a day. Must have gotten up to five, maybe six."

"How long have you been getting sick?"

A sharp pain stabbed at his side, and he grimaced. "Awhile. Right after we met."

"My poor darling. You've been suffering all this time and never let on." Melody scanned the room. "Where is that remedy? Let me get you some more."

He held his stomach in pain. "There is no more."

"What can I do?"

"There's nothing you can do. It usually goes away after a while. I'll be fine alone."

"Well, I'm not going to leave you alone. Not now. Not ever."

He tried to sit up, but the pain held him down. "What are you saying?"

"What I should have said last night. I don't care who or what you are. I love you. And nothing will ever change that."

He touched the side of her face with his fingertip. He'd never get over the silkiness of her skin. "You don't know what you're saying."

"For the first time in my life, I know exactly what I'm saying." She leaned over farther and whispered in his ear, "I just have one question for you, Count. What's it like being a vampire?"

"It's a very lonely existence unless you have someone to share it with." His gaze locked with hers.

"My thoughts exactly." Her eyes smiled back at him.

"You would do that for me?"

"Absolutely. I'm willing to compromise."

He curled his arm around her neck and pulled her down on top of him. His mouth found hers, and he kissed her with all the joy he felt in his heart.

"Ah, hmmm." Sugar cleared her throat. "I don't mean to interrupt you two lovebirds, but—" She tapped her watch. "It's getting late."

Melody looked over at her. "You're right. I'd better get dressed." Then she turned her attention back to him. "And you, can you make it to the elimination ceremony?"

"Nothing on earth would stop me."

She kissed him again, then pulled back and studied him. "You're so unnaturally pale today. We have to do something with your skin." Melody's gaze went to the doorway. She motioned for Sugar to come inside.

"Guy's not feeling well. Would you put some makeup on him to give him some color?" she asked.

Sugar winked. "Of course, hon, that is my job, after all."

"Thanks. I'll see you both at the beach, pronto." Melody blew Guystof a kiss good-bye and dashed from his *bure*.

He sat up in bed and watched Sugar set up her makeup case. She pulled out a tube, squeezed some flesh-colored cream into her palm, then came over to him and, with a small sponge, applied it to his face. He didn't especially like the feel of it on his skin, but if it helped make him look normal, he'd put up with it.

When Sugar finished with him, she handed him a mirror, and to his surprise, he looked remarkably healthy. "You've done a fine job. I don't know how to thank you."

"Just take care of my girl," she warned.

Guystof wished he could promise her he would, but that wouldn't be the truth. He was a vampire and knew well the dangers that came along with that. The most he could say was, "I'll do my best."

ଛଡ଼

Melody felt very much a princess as she sat on her throne-like chair on top the bamboo sea raft that carried her to the bachelors. The ocean was quiet and looked like blue glass. She watched as her *bure* disappeared from view and felt a twinge of sadness, knowing come this time tomorrow she'd be leaving Fiji.

A sea turtle swam by, its head lifted above the water as if to warm it in the bright afternoon sun. She thought back to all the things she'd seen and done during her stay on this tropical island paradise—visiting the rainforest, snorkeling in the warm Pacific Ocean, and drinking kava with the natives. All things that just a short while ago she'd never imagined she'd experience.

However, when she spotted the men on the beach looking chic in their formal attire, she left her nostalgia behind. She caught sight of Guy, tall and suave and by far the most handsome bachelor. Her breath caught in her throat. Soon the world would know that not only was she his dream girl, but he was the man of her dreams.

Four warriors dressed in native Fijian attire brought the raft to shore. One offered her his hand and helped her off. He walked her to the ceremonial spot, a lovely area shaded from the sun by palm trees and ferns. A cool trade wind blew from the southeast and ruffled her hair. She took a deep breath, folded her hands in front of her, and waited for Henry to come forward.

He smiled at her and took his place at her side. "Are you ready?"

She nodded, and he looked out over the men. "Well, this is what you've all been waiting for. Melody is ready to announce the name of the bachelor she's chosen." He kissed her cheek, then stepped back out of the limelight.

Melody squeezed her hands together to steady their trembling. She didn't know why she was nervous. She shouldn't be. There was no doubt in her mind whose name she would call. But for some reason that knowledge did nothing to quell her rapid heartbeat. She closed her eyes. This was a big step. No, a huge one. But one she'd been waiting a lifetime for.

When she opened her eyes, she focused on the man with the cropped black hair, and her nervousness disappeared. His vibrant blue eyes told her everything would be all right.

She offered him a wide smile, then said in a loud, clear voice, "Guy LeBreque, will you accept this lei?" She took the fresh flower lei from the arm of a warrior and held it out in front of her.

Guy came forward faster than she expected—a good indication that he was feeling better—took her by the waist and twirled her around.

"I'll take that as a yes." She laughed.

"Positively." He tipped his head, and she draped the lei around his neck. His mouth sought hers, and he kissed her. Cheers and clapping ensued. Their lips parted, and they looked out at the group of well-wishers—Henry, Sugar, the crew, even the other bachelors cheered and seemed genuinely happy for them.

Serenie and her boys emerged from the crowd. They carried a baby coconut tree. Serenie set it down in front of Melody and Guy.

"This tree will be planted here," she said in her melodic voice, "with a sign inscribed with both your names, so that the tree may grow with your love."

Melody hugged Serenie, thanking her for such a thoughtful gift, then she took hold of Guy's hand and together they walked down the beach in the direction of her *bure*.

Behind them, she heard Daniel yell, "It's a wrap, folks." The crowd roared, and Melody didn't need to turn around to know the cameraman slowly faded them to black as they walked away into the sunset.

Guy draped his arm around her shoulders, and she snuggled against him, feeling happy and cherished and deeply in love. While they walked, they watched the sun set behind the horizon. The sky, awash with brilliant color, was streaked with magenta and purple, then dusk took hold and the first stars of the night winked above them.

They watched the sky turn black and a chill blew in from the water, but Melody barely felt it wrapped in the warmth of Guy's arms.

"Look!" He pointed up at the stars. "Do you see it? The Southern Cross."

She shook her head.

Gently, he cupped his hands around her head and guided her. "There."

"Oh, yes, I see it now. It's lovely."

"It sure is." His gaze was directed on her, though.

Her cheeks warmed and she looked back up at the sky. "In times gone by, it was used by travelers as a guide."

"Do you think it will help us?"

"Do what? Find our way home?"

"Perhaps."

"I don't think we'll need it." She swung around. "'Cause we're already there." She laughed and started to run across the sand, then called over her shoulder, "Come on, pokey, I'll race you."

He needed no more prompting. Soon, they were side by side; then with a burst of speed he sprinted ahead. When he reached the *bure* door, he yanked it open but waited on the threshold for her to catch up.

"Allow me." He swept her into his arms and carried her inside, depositing her on the bed and collapsing beside her, where he lay laughing and trying to catch his breath.

Melody had never seen Guy so playful. It was a side of him he'd never shown her before and one she hoped to see a lot more of.

"I can't wait to introduce you to everyone back home. I know they'll adore you just as much as I do." She lay on her back, crossed one leg over the other and stared up at the ceiling with a huge grin on her face; then she reached out and stroked the side of his face. "And I know you'll like them. Now Ann, she's my best friend and an awful lot like me, just a little quirkier. And Mags and Billy. They're so much fun. And Gizmo. Oh, how I miss him. He's my dog—"

The look on Guy's face made her snap her mouth shut. "What's wrong? What did I say?"

He took hold of her hand and brought it to his mouth, running his lips over her palm. "You did nothing, love. In fact, I've never seen you quite so animated as you were when you spoke of those you love."

She frowned, not quite sure what he was getting at. "Sooo?"

He looked at her mournfully. "Have you forgotten what I am?

What you've promised to become?"

The blood raced from her head down into her toes, and she had no doubt that she was as pale as a ghost. "Ah, no, not forgotten, just kind of shelved to the back of my mind."

"I'm serious, Melody."

She rolled onto her side and propped her head up with her hand so that she stared straight into his crystal-blue eyes. "I know you are. I got caught up in the excitement of us, that's all. But I haven't forgotten, nor would I ever take back the promise I made to you. We were meant to be together. I'm sure of that. And if that means I have to become a vampire, then I will." She offered him a smile despite the melancholy that flooded her. What if she never saw her family again…or Gizmo…or the girls?

As if reading her mood and wanting to shake her free of it, he pulled her to her feet and led her to the french doors, where outside on the patio a candlelit dinner awaited them.

Melody's eyes widened in disbelief. "Did you do this?"

A smile curved his full lips and he said, slipping into his sexy Romanian accent, "Sometimes a little bit of magic comes in handy."

"That it does." She stepped outside and walked over to the table, sparkling with crystal and china and overflowing with enough food to feed the entire *Dream Girl* crew.

"You shouldn't have gone to so much trouble for only the two of us."

"It was no trouble, my love. A little point of the finger here, a little snap there, and voilá, you have a feast. Besides," he said, removing a stem of grapes from the fruit bowl in the center of the table, "I had more in mind than simply eating dinner when I created this."

"Oh!"

He tore a grape off the stem, ran it across her lips, then teased her with it until she opened her mouth. Her teeth pierced the grape, and its succulent juice exploded in her mouth. The next thing she knew, his lips were on hers.

He burned a trail of fire over her skin as he caressed her neck. Slowly he slid one strap of her gold lame shell down off her shoulder, then the other. He touched her breasts until her nipples grew hard, then with nimble fingers undid her sarong, so both her top and bottom fell in a heap of shimmering gold at her feet. She stood before him, nearly naked, in only her under garments, yet she was not ashamed.

He gazed at her with such open admiration that she felt like the most beautiful woman alive.

"You are lovelier than I ever imagined." He ran his forefinger from the base of her neck to just below her navel, sending erotic shivers down her spine.

"Looks like dinner is going to have to wait." He lifted her in his arms and carried her across the patio, setting her back on her feet in front of the hot tub. "This is just much too enticing." He reached behind her back and undid the hooks to her bra, slipping the straps off so that he held the lace undergarment in his hands.

Her instincts were to cover herself, but he held her arms at her sides so that he might look at her. Then he let her go and cupped both her breasts in his hands and squeezed gently.

Moans of delight escaped her, and she arched her back as he slid his warm, soft mouth over her skin and sucked her nipple. With his hands, he traced her body, running them down her back, over her hips, and up along her thighs until she wiggled with pleasure.

"Ah, you like that, do you?" He touched the spot between her legs that had grown wet with desire, then rubbed his fingers over her silky panties until she thought she was going to scream.

"Not yet, my love, the night is young." He looped his fingers around the sides of her panties and pulled them down.

Totally naked now and trembling with passion, she wanted him more than she could have imagined. Yet, he teased and played with her while he remained fully clothed. She wrapped her arms around him, pressing her body against his so the thunderous beat of his heart rang in her ear.

He massaged the small of her back, then slid his hands down to her tailbone and over her bottom, where he held her tightly as she moved against his thigh. The bulge in his pants grew larger and harder. And just when she thought she couldn't take it anymore, he took her hand and urged her into the Jacuzzi. He watched her step into the hot, bubbling water, and the way he looked at her made her tremble some more.

She sank down, letting the water come up to just under her chin. The jets pulsated shots of water all around her and she relaxed in the tub while she watched Guy undress.

She bit her bottom lip and studied this exquisite man—tall and lean and with muscles rippling in places she hadn't even known existed—as he stripped off his clothes. She opened her arms to him and watched him enter the water with the sexy stride of a jungle cat.

He came to her and straddled her, gripping the edges of the hot tub. She caressed his strong, muscular chest, then touched his flat, six-pack belly. She curled her arms around his back and he lifted her up out of the water and sat her on his lap. Hot water lapped over her breasts, soothing her. She leaned back and closed her eyes while Guy worked magic with his hands.

ജ്ഞ

Melody lay across Guystof, her head resting against the edge of the hot tub and her soft round bottom pressing against his legs. He tickled the insides of her thighs, and when she squirmed, he wasn't sure how much longer he'd be able to hold back.

She was everything he'd dreamed of and more, this golden goddess. And tonight she would be his. He knew he could have her now. She was more than ready. Gently, he spread her legs, rubbing and tickling until he could slide two fingers inside her easily. Oh yes. She was indeed ready. But he didn't want to rush things, this being her first time. He wanted this to be a night she would remember always.

He studied her from the tips of her perfectly manicured toes to the top of her lovely head. Bathed in pale moonlight, she could not be more glorious. He was a lucky man. A lucky man indeed. The graceful sweep of her neck seemed bare without his kisses. As he leaned over to taste her skin, the pinch of his fangs broke through his gums and stopped him.

What was happening? Surely the potion he'd taken could last one more day. He wasn't ready to turn her. Not here. Not now. After they'd said their vows and were man and wife, that would be the correct time. When they were home at Dragesa, where he could make her comfortable and help her through the pain. It would not be easy for Melody to lose her mortal life and become a vampire.

He turned his head and fought the ever growing desire to bite her, to taste her sweet blood trickle down his throat, quenching the hunger inside him. He'd never sunk his fangs into a woman before and to do so now, to his beloved… He squeezed his eyes shut and pushed her away.

"What is it? Has your sickness returned?"

Guystof looked at her, concern and worry reflected in her eyes. "Yes. I'm ill. You should go get dressed."

"Why? Let me help you." She ran the back of her hand over his forehead.

He grabbed her arm and held it away from him. "I don't need your help."

Her eyes darkened with despair. "Why are you doing this? Why are you pushing me away? If I'm going to be your wife, you have to open up to me."

Gut-wrenching pain shot through him, and he hunched over. "I don't have the strength to argue with you now. Do as I say and go."

Water bubbled up around her waist as she stood before him with her hands planted firmly on her hips. "I'm not used to being ordered around. And I will not leave you, especially when you're sick."

Anger and pain coursed through him and erupted in a roar. "Melody!"

She backed up, the wall of the hot tub keeping her from going any farther. Her eyes were wide and full of shock as she stared dumbfounded at his mouth.

He ran his hand over his teeth and felt the fangs protruding from his gums. In a thickened voice he begged, "Please, please, just go."

Her eyes softened, and her gaze locked with his. "That's what's causing you so much pain. You need to feed." She came toward him, then tilted her head and pulled back her hair, offering him her neck.

Shock and amazement froze him.

"Go on. Do it."

He touched her throat with his finger, then leaned in, saliva burning his tongue, tempting him to make the kill. He opened his mouth, his teeth pressed against her pearly neck. Just moments away from piercing the artery showing beneath her skin, a pain more horrible than ever before stopped him. But it wasn't his stomach that hurt. It was his chest. He loved her too much to be so selfish. He raised his head and looked at her. "I can't."

Melody let her hair swing back over her shoulders. "Are you sure?"

He nodded. "We must wait until we get to Moldavia. I don't

want to hurt you, or at least to cause you any more pain than is absolutely necessary."

"I see. I guess I'll go get dressed then." She stepped out of the Jacuzzi and wrapped a towel around herself, covering her nakedness.

Perhaps from him? "Are you rethinking all this?" he asked.

"No. Not at all." She twisted her hair to remove the water. "I just don't like to think about it being painful, that's all."

"Do you have a cross?"

She raised her brows at him. "Yes. Yes, I do. In my purse."

"Well, go and get it."

"Why?"

"To protect you from me."

"Oh!" Melody raced through the french doors, returning in no time with a tiny gold cross dangling from her fingers. "Ann loaned me this. She said it would keep me safe."

"Thank goodness for Ann," Guystof said. "Now put it on. And whatever you do, don't take it off."

CHAPTER TEN

Melody slept through most of the flight to Moldavia. After last night and this morning's emotional farewell to the *Dream Girl* crew, not only was she physically exhausted but mentally too. There was no doubt she was going to miss Sugar. The busty redhead had become so much more than her hairdresser and makeup artist. She'd become her friend and confidant. Who would she share girl-talk with now?

She cast a sideways glance at Guy, who sat silently, staring out the window of the limo as they drove toward Dragesa. This country, with its bleak, stark landscape, was nothing like Fiji. She felt like she'd been taken back in time hundreds of years. They passed peasants working in fields, who stopped what they were doing to stare at the car, their faces prematurely wrinkled due to their hard lives and their eyes darkened with fear. She wondered what they must be thinking of their master—that was what Guy was, wasn't he?—as he drove past them in his luxurious vehicle, while most of them probably didn't even own a car. Was he kind to them? Or was he a fierce taskmaster?

She realized she knew next to nothing about him. Well, other than that he was a vampire, of course. She fingered the cross around her neck, seeking comfort in its presence. It wasn't that she regretted her decision to come here. She loved Guy. It was just this whole vampire thing would take some getting used to.

On Fiji, it hadn't seemed real, even when she'd offered to let him sink his fangs into her, but here against this backdrop, reality had hit her as fast as the dank, cold fog that met her when she stepped off the plane.

She leaned back against the leather seat and closed her eyes. She wished Gizmo was there with her, rubbing his wet nose on her hand. And Ann. Oh, how she missed having her best friend to talk to. Melody started when Guy patted her arm.

"We're almost there," he announced.

She looked out the window. They were fast approaching a vast gray stone castle perched on the side of a cliff. Although it was dusk, no light came from its tall black windows, and its broken battlements showed a jagged line against the evening sky. She imagined unmentionable horrors coming from behind locked doors—screams going unheard and echoing throughout its chambers.

"So what do you think of my home?"

She pulled her gaze away and looked at Guy. "It's big."

"I probably shouldn't have asked until you've had a chance to see the inside."

She pasted on a smile. "That's a good idea. It's kind of overwhelming."

The limousine pulled up the circular drive and stopped in front of a massive wood door. The driver got out and opened her door, then went around to the trunk and removed their luggage. Guy came over and offered her his hand and helped her out. Servants had lined up along the cobblestone walkway, their heads bowed, waiting for Guy to acknowledge them.

"Good day. I trust everything is in order?"

A plump middle-aged woman with short, wiry hair that curled around her face like little silver springs stepped forward. "Indeed, sir. And glad to finally have you home. Your father is awaiting you in his study."

"Thank you, Clarisse."

She offered up a small curtsey, then stepped back in line.

An elderly gentleman with salt-and-pepper hair approached Guy next. He had a stilted gait, yet moved with dignity. His gaze swept over Melody boldly, indicating he was more than a servant.

He gave Guy a hearty handshake and a wide smile. "I've missed you, sir." He looked back at her, then winked at Guy. "I had a room prepared for the mistress. Shall I take her up?"

Guy clapped the old man on the back. "You think of everything."

"I try to, sir."

She crossed her arms, a little peeved that they'd been so sure she'd choose Guy as her bachelor, but when he looked at her, his blue eyes sparkling, his pleasure at being home so evident, her irritation faded.

"Melody, this is Blakesley. He's like a surrogate father to me." He placed his arm around her waist. "And this is Miss Melody Johnson, my soon-to-be wife."

Blakesley bowed slightly, lifted her hand, and kissed it. "Pleasure to meet you, miss."

"Thank you." She glanced over the top of his head at the servants behind him, all chattering gaily. It was evident they thought highly of their master and were pleased he'd found a bride.

"Now that the introductions are over with, I'm sure Melody would like to freshen up a bit," Guy instructed.

"Right this way, Miss Melody." Blakesley held the door open for her.

She looked over at Guy. "I'm fine, really. I'd much rather stay with you."

The servants gasped, and Guy frowned. There was no denying his disapproval at her objection.

"You know what. I do need to freshen up." She covered her mouth to stifle a pretend yawn. "And I'm feeling a little tired too. Please excuse me." She followed Blakesley inside and felt like the heroine in a B-movie.

A musty smell permeated the castle. The only light glowed from candles flickering eerily against high stone walls, changing shape and casting shadows where none should have been. Was it too much to hope this was done simply for effect? "No electricity?"

"I hope that won't be an inconvenience for you." Blakesley led her up a long, winding staircase.

"Oh, of course not," she said sweetly, then mumbled under her breath, "If I'm going to be a vampire, I guess I'd better get used to the dark."

Blakesley turned and looked down at her. "Did you say something, miss?"

She ran her hand over a flocked wall covering, fingering a hole chewed away, no doubt by mice. "I was just admiring the tapestry."

"It's quite old. Dates back centuries."

Along with everything else in this place. It's not that she didn't appreciate antiques, but this place was just downright creepy.

They came to the top of the stairs and headed down a narrow, dimly lit passage.

Blakesley unlocked a door, then pushed it open. "Here you are, miss. I hope it's to your liking."

And if it's not, will you let me stay with Guy? "I'm sure it'll be fine." She stepped inside and wanted to bite back her words. If this was where they put the master's bride, what did the other rooms look like?

A large four-poster bed encircled with worn red velvet draperies caught her eye first. Beside it, she noticed an overstuffed chair with the same gaudy fabric, and an ornate carving that covered the high wooden back. A stuffed bird of some sort with long black feathers stared at her with beady eyes.

"I'll have your bags sent right up, miss."

Melody forced a smile. "Thank you. I'd appreciate that."

Blakesley closed the door halfway, poking his head back inside. "Oh, and miss?"

"Yes?"

"I'm pleased that you've come. I hope that you'll be happy with the count. He's a fine man." Blakesley closed the door softly, and she heard his footsteps disappear down the hall.

Guy was a fine man, and that thought helped to cheer her as she plopped onto the bed. A dust cloud encircled her. She covered her mouth while she coughed. What had she been thinking when she agreed to come here? Well, she knew one thing for certain. If she was going to live here, this place was getting a makeover.

She strolled over to a tarnished wall mirror and raked her fingers through her hair. Guy had been right. She did need to freshen up. Melody checked out the adjoining bathroom and prayed there'd be running water. When she turned the faucet, she was greeted with a trickle and some rust, so she let the bathwater run until it turned clear before she put the stopper in. A few minutes later, it was near to overflowing. She leaned over, turned off the water, and Ann's gold cross dropped into the tub. Lucky she had the plug in, she thought, fishing it out. She set it on the sink to dry as a knock sounded at her door. Must be her suitcases, at last.

She went back into the bedroom and swung the door open. Her heart did a flip-flop. No servant stood before her. It was the sexy

Romanian with the curly blond hair and deep chocolate eyes. Guy's brother.

ଛଚ

"Melody, it's so nice to see you again." Theo smiled broadly and pushed past her before she could slam the door on him.

"What do you want?" She glared at him, fear evident in her gorgeous eyes.

He reached out and took hold of her hand, bringing it up to his mouth. He ran his lips over her soft, smooth skin before kissing it.

She pulled back, wiping her hand on her jeans. "Get out!"

Theo laughed at her attempt to order him, as if her words would cause him to leave. "My dear, why on earth would I do that when I've only just arrived?"

"Guy will be here any second, and he won't be happy to find you in my room."

He chuckled again. "Is that what you call him? Guy? How very endearing."

"That's not his name?"

"Well, yes, I suppose it is. I've just never heard anyone call him that before. He's known here as Guystof."

She glared at him. "As I said, Guy will not be happy to find you in my room."

"Don't worry, I'm not staying. And neither are you."

"What?" She took a step toward the door, but he grabbed hold of her arm, pulling her to him.

"Ah, you don't think I'd let you go, now do you?"

She pummeled his chest with her fist.

"While I do find your resistance arousing, I can't have you fighting me right now." He pulled a white linen handkerchief from his pocket and placed it under her nose. Her body relaxed, and she fell against him, limp as a rag doll.

He carried her out of the room. Melody's golden hair fell in long spirals over his arm. Her lashes fanned the tops of her high cheekbones, and her facial muscles were relaxed as if she were merely asleep. It would be quite some time before she woke, though. Theo was very familiar with the drug he'd used on her. The root of the tamerine plant, mixed with some ten other herbs, made a powerful sedative when inhaled. He'd been using the concoction for centuries on women he planned to turn into vampires and add to his harem.

He zigzagged through the dark corridors easily, for he knew them well. Soon, he came to a wing of the castle which hadn't been used for centuries. When he came to a narrow stairwell, he stepped carefully down the slick, mold-covered stairs. At the bottom, he used his magic to open a trapdoor in the floor. The passage was low, and Theo had to crouch as he walked.

It was a relief when he reached the cavern with its twenty-foot ceiling. He placed Melody down gently at the edge of an underground lake. Ripples broke the surface of the otherwise still water, and he watched the red-haired beauty row a small boat toward him. Saliva formed in his mouth, and his fangs broke through his gum line.

Gelda brought the boat ashore and stepped out gracefully. It took all his willpower to keep from sinking his teeth into her sweet flesh. She took great pleasure in being fed upon, but today, despite how tempting the vampire might be, he had more important matters to attend to.

"A new member of our family?" Gelda's brows rose as her gaze scanned over Melody.

"She will be soon. I need you to prepare her for the turning ceremony."

Gelda smiled, exposing long, pearly fangs. "With pleasure." She reached for Melody, but Theo caught her by the waist first.

"Not so fast. There's no hurry. The girl won't wake for a while yet." He ran his hands down Gelda's muscular back. He'd almost forgotten how good she felt.

She purred with delight, and he teased her further by tracing his fingertip over her collarbone.

When she lifted up her hair, offering him her long, slender neck, he whispered in her ear, "Not now, love. There'll be time for that later. Just checking to make sure you haven't forgotten me."

She kissed his cheek, then moved her mouth down, letting the tip of her fang press into his throat. "Never," she whispered back.

"Good. Would be a pity to have to kill you."

She laughed, but he knew she was fully aware that he wasn't joking. Theo had killed vampires in his harem before. If one of them fell out of favor, he would let the others feed upon her until they had drained the offender of all blood.

He kissed Gelda's soft lips before releasing her. "Have Melody ready at midnight."

෨෬

Guystof leaned back in the leather chair, sipped a cup of tea—Earl Grey, black no sugar—and studied his father. A usually robust man, he now looked haggard. Dark bags hung beneath his clear blue eyes, the same shade of blue as Guystof's. He came around the large mahogany desk that separated them and placed his hands on Guystof's shoulders. "Have you some news for me, son?"

"Ah, you've been dying to ask, haven't you?" With a chuckle, he set his teacup on the table. "Indeed I do. News that will be sure to please you."

"Dare I wager a bet on what it is?" He offered his son a tired smile. "Or should I simply ask her name?"

Guystof placed a hand over his father's and squeezed. "It's Melody Johnson. And you're going to love her."

"If you do, then I shall too. Besides, it will be nice to have a daughter finally after all these years." He walked over to the wall that held a row of family portraits and scanned each of them, stopping when he came to Guystof's mother. "I loved her very much. She was a mortal too. Just like your Melody." His voice was low, as if he spoke only to himself. "It's a difficult path for them—those mortals who chose to become like us. Especially for woman. Painful. Right at the start and at the end."

Guystof's father was thinking back to long ago, rehashing old wounds. It would serve him no good, though he had to admit he'd also been thinking of his mother and of her death... No matter what, he would not let that happen to Melody. He would watch over her night and day. "Shall I bring her to you?"

"I can see you're anxious to show her off, but we have some business to attend to first."

Guystof knew exactly to what he referred. Dragesa. His legacy.

His father pulled a document from his desk drawer and smoothed the curled parchment with his hands. "Although I love Theo, he is my son, too, but he is not the rightful heir to the kingdom and would make a terrible ruler to boot. Much too selfish." His father took out a feather pen and dipped it in the well. "And since you have fulfilled your obligation and have chosen a bride, I see no reason to wait any longer." He scribbled his name at the bottom, then handed the pen to his son.

Guystof set it down on the table. "But you can't be ready to retire. Not yet."

His father picked it up and slipped it into Guystof's hand. "My rule is finished. It's time for a future generation to take over. A kinder, more considerate one." Lines crinkled around the corners of his eyes as he smiled.

Guystof smiled back and put his signature beside his father's.

"Well, son, all that's required now to make it legal is the royal seal. We'll set that upon it on your wedding day." His father rolled the document back up. "And we mustn't forget this." He reached into the neckline of his cape and pulled out a black leather cord, on which hung a gold lion-head pendant. He took off the necklace, then put it around Guystof's neck. "Now let's have a look at that bride-to-be of yours."

"Yes, sir." Guystof raced out of the study and nearly bumped into Blakesley in the great hall.

"May I assume everything went well with your father, sir?"

Guystof flashed him a huge smile. "Indeed you may." He bounded up the staircase two steps at a time. When halfway up, he turned and looked down over his shoulder. "Which room is—"

"Third floor, last door on your right," Blakesley said, before he could finish asking the question.

Guystof raced up the rest of the stairs, then down the long, narrow hall. He couldn't wait to tell Melody the news. Dragesa was almost his, and that meant Theo's days of lying and cheating to get what he wanted were over. He would now have to abide by a new set of rules—Guystof's rules.

Although out of breath when he reached Melody's room, that didn't take away his excitement about the future. Their future together. He knocked on her door. After getting no answer, he opened it a crack and peeked inside.

The room was dark. Only the glow of moonlight shining in through the window provided any light. His gaze immediately focused on the four-poster bed. The velvet draperies around it were closed. Poor darling. She must have fallen asleep. He could tell she'd been exhausted by their long trip. He contemplated whether to wake her or leave her to sleep a while longer, but a young servant boy arrived with her luggage and made such a racquet surely she'd wake on her own.

But she didn't. What a sound sleeper she was! He stepped over to the bed and drew back the drapery. His chest tightened. The pounding of his heart thrummed in his ears. The bed was empty.

"Melody!" He looked around the room, then over to the bathroom. The door was ajar. He strode over to it in three large strides and pushed it open. The tiny room was empty. A glint of gold caught his eye. Melody's cross lay on the edge of the sink. "I told you to never take it off."

A murderous rage filled him. There was no doubt in his mind Theo had taken her. But where?

"If you hurt her in any way, brother, you will pay dearly," he shouted at the empty room.

CHAPTER ELEVEN

Melody's body ached. Her head pounded. When she opened her eyes, the room spun. A wave of nausea took hold, and she fought back the need to vomit. What in the world had happened to her? She blinked a few times to bring the room into focus. An eerie world of stalactites and stalagmites sparkled in the light of dozens of candles. Their flames eerily danced and flickered over slime-covered stone walls. A damp, moldy smell permeated her nose. Where the heck was she? Melody tried to sit up, but steel clamps held her wrists and ankles to a limestone table.

Her cloudy memory began to clear. The last thing she remembered was seeing Theo's evil face. She shivered, not just from cold but at the thought of that monster. It was then that she realized she was naked. What happened to her clothes? Worse yet, who had taken them off her? Her stomach churned when she thought it may have been Theo.

"Help!" Her scream echoed through the cave. "Please, someone, anyone. Help me."

From the shadows, a tall, Amazon-like woman approached. Her bright red hair was sleek and bobbed with short straight bangs that showed off dark, finely arched brows. The effect made her pale skin look alabaster. On top of her head, worn like a band, were silver goggles with a skull and crossbones etched in each eyepiece. She wore a black lace corset, baggy trousers tucked inside tall, shiny platform boots with lots of buckles. The woman was reminiscent of a 1920's Amelia Earhart with a weird Goth twist. Her green eyes were rimmed with black liner, and they glistened like emeralds. Her full, blood-red lips curved up at the corners, not in a smile exactly, more like a smirk, and exposed a pair of pearly fangs. In her hands she held a black velvet robe.

"It will do you no good to scream. Only make your head ache more." Her voice was low-pitched and gravelly.

"Who are you? And how do you know my head hurts?"

The woman raised a pencil-thin brow. "The drug you were given is very powerful. It makes everything hurt."

"Please, let me go. Guy—Guystof—heir to this whole kingdom—and I are going to be married. If you help me, I'll see that you're rewarded."

"Melody, you are so naïve."

"You know my name?"

The woman laughed. "I know everything about you. And I know you are not going to marry the count, nor is he going to inherit Dragesa."

"And how do you know that?"

"Because if he doesn't marry you or some other rich woman by the end of this week, Theo inherits it all."

She knew that. Guy had confessed everything. "You're wrong. Guy loves me. Truly loves me."

The woman dropped the robe and came to stand beside her. Using her pointer finger, she ran the tip of her long, red nail over Melody's arm. "Oh, poor thing. You really do believe he was going to marry you for love."

Of course she did, but maybe she could use the woman's words to her advantage and play along with her. "Maybe I shouldn't have believed him. If I promise not to marry him, will you let me go?"

Her red lips curled, almost into a snarl. "Of course not. Disobey Theo and risk my own life? I think not."

"Then at least tell me what's going to happen."

"You want to know your future?"

"Yes."

"You're going to become one of us."

"A vampire?"

"Not just a vampire. Part of Theo's harem. Now shut up so I can prepare you for tonight's ceremony."

"Tonight? Ceremony?" Melody tried not to let her voice quiver, but fear shook her.

"Quiet!"

The woman walked out of view, and Melody thought perhaps she'd left the cave, but a few seconds later, she was back, carrying a gun. Oh Lord! The crazy vampire was going to shoot her. Melody's heart skipped a beat. "Please, don't shoot me. I promise to keep quiet. I won't say another word."

"Good."

But to Melody's horror, she took aim at her and pulled the trigger. Melody squeezed her eyes shut. In that tenth of a second before the bullet hit, her life flashed before her. She saw her mom and dad, Billy, Mags, Ann, and Gizmo. Thank goodness her friends would take care of her dog.

The last face she saw before the bullet's scathing sting was Guy's. Her impending death didn't seem as tragic as the fact that she'd never see him again. They wouldn't marry, and they'd never make love. A heaviness tightened her chest, and along with that, she felt blood—her blood—trickle down her side. Then the vampire's hot breath was near her ear. What was she going to do now, finish Melody off with a bite to the neck? Afraid to look yet more afraid not to, she opened her eyes a sliver. A scream welled up in her throat at the sight of long fangs inches from her body. Oh, please, let it be over fast. Don't make me suffer, she prayed, shutting her eyes again.

Blood spread over her stomach and down her thighs. She risked another peek. White? Her blood was white. She turned her head to the side, and to her surprise, the vampire was holding a large paintbrush.

"Did you think I was going to kill you?"

Melody nodded.

"Although I would love to—I am famished—that pleasure belongs to Theo. My job is to ready you for him. I shot you with a paint pellet."

"Why?"

"Theo likes his women white. Extremely white." She moved the brush along Melody's legs, then over her arms and hands. She painted her face, even her eyebrows. By the time she moved on to Melody's feet, her body was dry and beginning to itch.

"Please. Will you undo my wrist? I need to scratch my nose," Melody pleaded.

"I'll do better than that. I'll unlock all the cuffs." She moved around Melody, unlocking each clamp. "Now turn over," she ordered, "but I warn you, if you try anything funny, I'll make you wish I had used a bullet."

Quickly, she itched the tip of her nose, then turned onto her stomach. In any other circumstance, she would have been mortified to be laid out naked, but right now her thoughts were solely on how to escape, and this was her opportunity.

She brought her elbow up, and, with all her strength, jabbed the vampire in the chest. The woman let out a howl of pain and grabbed her breasts.

There were numerous passages out of the cave, and Melody didn't hesitate in selecting one. She didn't know she could run so fast and over slick limestone, too, but there was no doubt the vampire was in close pursuit. She couldn't let up, not even for a second. Melody ran down the dark passage, not knowing or caring where she was headed. Eventually she was bound to find her way out.

After what seemed like hours, the passage split. No footsteps rang out behind her, so she stopped to catch her breath before selecting which way to go. She leaned over and placed her hands on her knees. Her tired gaze rested on a pair of black leather boots, then slowly moved up to perfectly cut pants that hugged well-muscled thighs, and on to a white linen shirt open at the chest, exposing a blanket of blond curly hair. Her gaze continued up until it locked with a pair of deep chocolate eyes.

Theo brought a well-manicured finger up to his mouth. "Let me see. Which way should you go, to the right or to the left?"

Melody stood straight and used her arms to try to cover her nakedness, but it was useless. She was thoroughly exposed to him, like an insect under a microscope.

When she opened her mouth to speak, Theo put his hand out silencing her. "How about you turn around and go back the way you came? It's bad luck for me to see my bride on our wedding day."

She gasped. "Bride?"

He reached out and drew a line across her collarbone with his finger. "You must know, my dear, I find you very attractive."

She shrank away from him, repulsed by his touch.

"Aw, what's wrong? You don't find me attractive?"

"You're a monster," she hissed. "I'll never marry you."

He moved closer to her. "I'm afraid you have no say. You'll be spending a very long time with me, like it or not."

"Never." She tried to back up, but he wrapped an arm around her waist, pressing her against him. Nausea gagged her.

"I won't lie to you. No matter what, tonight's ceremony will be painful, but it's your choice as to what happens after that." He ran his mouth along the side of her neck, then held her out at arms' length. "We can spend forever as partners, or you can join my harem and serve my every whim, and, I assure you, there won't be an ounce of pleasure in that…for you."

By the way his gaze scoured her body, she knew he would have his way with her, even if she did cooperate. "You might be able to control my destiny, but you'll never have my love."

His laugh was so evil it made her shudder. "Are you really that naïve? Do you think I care or want love?" He took her by the shoulders, spun her around, and murmured at her back, "My soft-hearted brother might think such emotions matter, but I have no use for them. Now, let's go. We have to finish your wedding preparation."

A figure emerged from the shadows. "Wedding?"

"Well, you finally arrived," Theo snapped. "If I hadn't intervened, Melody may have found her way out of the caves."

The red-haired vampire stepped forward to stand boldly before him. "You never said anything about marriage. Only a turning ceremony."

He pulled the vampire to him. "Since when do I have to fill you in on all my plans, Gelda?"

Her green eyes smoldered. "I don't care what you do with that mortal, so long as you don't marry her."

He grabbed a handful of her hair and yanked her head back. "When I want your opinion, I'll ask for it. It will serve you well to remember that." He let go of her hair and rubbed the back of her head. "There's no need for jealousy, my dear. You know I adore you. No other woman will ever change that."

Gelda covered his mouth with hers.

Melody felt like a voyeur watching them kiss. Their passion for each other was palpable. She inched back, thinking this would be a good time to make a run for it.

Theo's fingers curled around her wrist and tightened like a vise. His lips parted from Gelda's. He shot Melody a steely stare. "And where do you think you're going? Don't underestimate me. I can have one eye on you and the other elsewhere." He kissed Gelda's cheek.

Melody seethed. "When Guy finds you, you'll be so sorry."

Theo chuckled. "We'll see about that."

෨෬

Guystof pushed past the young servant boy who'd carried in Melody's luggage, nearly knocking him to the ground. He raced toward Theo's quarters in the north tower, not expecting to find him there but hoping to uncover a clue that would help lead him to Melody.

He burst into Theo's study and searched his desk, finding nothing of interest except some vials of potion in the bottom drawer. Had he drugged Melody? Guystof took one out and threw it at the wall. The vial shattered. A putrid green liquid sprayed out, creating a mottled mess on the wall. He picked up another vial and took aim.

"Sir, might I ask what you're doing?"

Guystof looked over his shoulder. Blakesley stood in the doorway. "The bastard has Melody." He threw the second vial.

"Then shouldn't we set out to find her?" The butler came to stand beside him and pushed the drawer shut.

"If I knew where she was, don't you think I'd already be there?" Guystof yanked open the drawer and hurled another vial at the wall.

"Sir, wouldn't it be wiser to take your frustration out in a more constructive way?"

"And how do you suggest I do that?"

"By using Theo's magic to your advantage." Blakesley pulled a key from his pants pocket. "I had this made some time ago, sir. I never trusted your brother, and since he always underestimated me, it wasn't difficult to borrow the master key and have a copy made." He strolled over to a gray metal cabinet and unlocked the door.

Guystof watched with interest. "Looks like Theo's misfortune shall be my gain."

"Indeed, sir." Blakesley took out a gem-encrusted gold chalice and a beaker of blood. He set the goblet on the desk, filled it with blood, then ran his hands over it and chanted, "*Plasa inca trea.* Show me where Theo has taken Melody."

Guystof peered into the blood as a vivid picture appeared. Melody lay captive on a limestone table while one of Theo's vampires painted her back white. "What is she doing?" He looked at Blakesley.

"I believe she's preparing Melody for the turning ceremony, sir."

Guystof gasped in horror. "It's against the rules for him to take my fiancée for his own pleasure."

"Have you ever known Theo to play fair in the past, sir?"

Certainly not, but he never expected his brother to go this far. How in the world did Theo expect to get away with it? Once Father found out, he would banish Theo from the kingdom. "Why would he turn Melody when all he has to do is keep her from me until next week? What could he possibly hope to gain by this?"

Blakesley pulled a handkerchief from his pocket and wiped his brow. "As you stated, sir, he cannot steal your fiancée for his own pleasure, but what if he were to marry her? That would be another matter."

"Damn." Guystof slammed his fists on the desk. "He wouldn't

dare."

"Now don't you underestimate him."

Guystof studied the picture inside the goblet more closely. Melody was held in a room full of strange, colorful formations and sparkling crystal pillars. "Do you have any idea where they are? Looks like they might be in a cave."

"There are caverns under the castle. Your grandfather used to practice his spells in them."

"What are we waiting for, then? Let's go." Guystof bolted for the door.

"Wait, sir." Blakesley hobbled after him. "I don't know how to get to them."

Guystof groaned. "What good is this knowledge if we can't use it to find Melody?"

Blakesley raked his fingers through his salt and pepper hair. "Just give me a moment, sir, and perhaps I'll be able to think of something that may be of help." He closed his eyes. "Each morning your grandfather would head off toward the unused wing of the castle. The entrance to the caves must be there somewhere."

Guystof took off at a gallop. If Theo managed to go through with the ceremony before Guystof found Melody, there would be nothing he could do. He took a lantern from the wall to help light his way through the unused wing's dark corridors. The musty smell nearly gagged him as he ran. When he came to a narrow stairway, he stopped and held the lantern out in front of him to illuminate the treacherous, mold-covered steps. Where those footprints in the mold? Theo's footprints? His heart thundered, and it took great restraint to keep from bolting down the stairs, but a careless step could land him headfirst at the bottom.

He treaded cautiously, following the footprints. They stopped a few feet from the bottom step. He knelt and studied the floor. With his fist, he knocked on it. As he'd suspected, a hollow sound rang out, and he ran his hand over the slick, moldy floor, feeling for the outline of a trapdoor. He located a chiseled notch that allowed him to slip his fingers under and lift up the door. Blakesley arrived as he was about to enter the underground passage.

"Impeccable timing, my friend." He smiled up at the old butler. "Watch yourself." He crouched to avoid hitting his head as he moved through the low tunnel.

After what seemed like an eternity in the dark, the passage opened up to a cave—an underground wonder full of mineral deposits in exquisite shapes, textures, and colors. Stalactites dripped down like icicles, while stalagmites rose up from the floor like giant swords. From the cave ceiling, delicate white spikes spread in all directions. A spectacular malachite-colored lake glistened. Guystof looked across it at the series of tunnels, and the joy he'd felt at coming this far dissolved. "What now?" he asked glumly. "She could've been taken down any one."

"You mustn't give up hope, sir."

"I wouldn't think of it." He ran his hand across his forehead. "I'll search every one of these tunnels if I have to and won't stop looking until I find Melody."

"I suppose we need to swim across the lake, sir." Blakesley looked apprehensively at the water.

"Not we, old man." Guystof handed the lantern to his butler. "This is the end of the road for you. You're not a strong enough swimmer to make it across safely."

"I can't leave you. Theo is dangerous."

"Precisely why I need you to go back to the castle. If I haven't returned with Melody by dawn, alert Father."

"I don't feel good about this. You don't know what you'll come up against."

"I appreciate your concern, but Theo won't harm me."

Blakesley looked at him skeptically. "I wouldn't put anything past that one, sir."

"Theo's ruthless, but he is my brother. I'll be fine." Guystof stepped up to the edge of the lake, then removed his shirt and shoes. "Wish me luck." He dove into the green water. As he swam, he carefully avoided the cloud-like rock formations just below the water's surface. When he reached the other side, he waved to Blakesley and watched the butler disappear into the passage that would lead him back to the castle; then Guystof chose which tunnel he hoped would take him to Melody.

He headed down a long, straight passage marred with deep fissures in the floor. To his dismay, the passage came to an abrupt end, and he was forced to turn around. Back at the lake, he chose another tunnel. He didn't have time for mistakes. Every wrong move put him at greater risk of losing Melody forever. He ran through the inky blackness, not caring that the tight flowstone walls scratched his arms. Up ahead, the dark was broken by an orange glow, and smoke cut through the dank smell. Torches! Could Melody be close?

༂ଠ୪

Melody tried to think of an escape plan as Gelda painted her back. But what could she do? She was a prisoner cuffed to a table. Would Guy rescue her in time? By now, he had to have discovered her missing.

The thought of marriage to Theo repulsed her. How could she ever have found him attractive? She remembered the day in the airport when she'd thought him beautiful. His looks were certainly deceiving. The handsome facade hid a monster. And she was going to have to spend centuries with him. A tear ran down her cheek.

"Don't be sad. Tonight is all about you, sweetie," Gelda said sarcastically.

An evil glint lit the vampire's cold eyes. She ran one more swipe of the paint brush over Melody's back, then admired her work like an artist would his painting. "As soon as you're dry, you can put on your ceremonial clothes. It won't be long before you'll become one of us." She let out a cackle, then disappeared from view.

"Are you still here?" Melody cried. Only the occasional drip of water from the walls onto the cave floor broke the ominous silence. The dampness made her shiver and the smell of mold and mildew turned her stomach. "Help! Can anyone hear me?" She screamed until her voice grew hoarse. It was no use. No one could hear, so no one would come. Guy wouldn't rescue her. She would be forced into a life of fear and darkness.

Footsteps interrupted her thoughts. Gelda appeared carrying an arm full of clothes and an elaborate headdress adorned with long black feathers. She placed the items on a mineralized pillar, then unshackled Melody.

"If you try any funny business, I promise you'll regret it," she warned.

Four large vampires emerged from the shadows and surrounded her.

"Put these on." Gelda threw the clothes at her.

After Melody slipped on the undergarments—black fishnet tights and a satin corset top—she stepped into a petticoat, over which she pulled a black knee-length skirt. Gelda handed her a pair of boots very much like the ones she wore; then a pair of vampires began applying makeup to her face, encircling her eyes with black liner. One drew a small red heart beneath her right eye. Another vampire draped the cape over her shoulders and tied the silk cord across her neckline. Someone else pinned her hair up, then placed the headpiece on top her head. It was heavy and toppled to the side. Gelda caught it before it hit the ground.

"Careful," she snapped, putting it back on Melody's head. "Theo would not be pleased if this were damaged." She took three tortoiseshell hairpins from a velvet pouch that hung from her wrist and used them to hold the headpiece steady.

Gelda took a step back and studied Melody carefully. "Almost perfect," she purred. "Just one more thing." She pulled a silver tube from the pouch and applied lipstick to Melody's mouth.

The consistency was different from any Melody had ever worn. She ran her tongue over her lips, not liking the tacky feel of it or the salty taste.

"You'll get used to it, my dear." Gelda handed her the tube.

She turned it over and read the label. Blood Red. Oh Lord! That wasn't just the color. There was blood in the lipstick. Her stomach churned, and she thought she might vomit. She rubbed at her mouth with the back of her hand.

Gelda laughed. "It won't come off that way. It's a stain. Has to wear off."

Melody dropped the tube. It rolled up against the limestone table. Gelda snapped her fingers, and a vampire took hold of each of Melody's arms. The others lit incense from the torches which lined the room. The strong smell of frankincense and sandalwood made her want to sneeze.

"Proceed," Gelda snapped.

They marched Melody toward a tunnel. She squeezed her eyes shut, not wanting to see or know what they had in store for her next.

CHAPTER TWELVE

M elody? Guystof swore he heard her cry for help. Although exhausted, he ran toward the torchlight. The tunnel opened up to a heavily perfumed cavern filled with a smoky haze. His excitement turned to dismay. Melody wasn't there. Could he have imagined hearing her voice? He scanned the room, his gaze landing on a limestone table with shackles attached to each end. He'd seen that table before. In Theo's magic goblet. His pulse raced. Melody had been there. He had heard her cry for help. It wasn't his imagination.

From the corner of his eye, he saw a flash of metal. On the floor lay a silver tube. He picked it up and opened the top. Lipstick. Blood-red lipstick. As a boy, he'd attended Tessa's turning ceremony. Blood-red lipstick was the final step in the preparation process. That could mean only one thing for Melody. It was just a matter of minutes before she would lose her mortal life.

Five tunnels led out of the cave and he had to choose the correct one. There was no time for a mistake. He rubbed his temples in an attempt to ease a pounding headache. It had to have been caused by that awful smell. What was it? The odor was vaguely familiar.

Incense! That too had been used in the turning ceremony. He raced over to a tunnel and inhaled deeply. The air was clear. He ran to another, and there was no mistaking the strong odor. Melody had to have been taken down that passage.

He dashed into the tunnel and was plunged into darkness. It took a little while for his eyes to adjust to the lack of light, so he felt his way by holding his arms out at his sides and feeling the tunnel walls. They were wet and slimy, but he didn't care. All he cared about was finding Melody. The incense smell was growing stronger with each step he took. Soon a pinpoint of light broke the darkness and he strode forward gingerly. He heard chanting. That could mean only one thing. The turning ceremony had begun, and afterward, Theo would make Melody his bride.

Guystof's blood boiled. It took all his willpower to keep from charging forward into the ceremony, but that would be the worst thing he could do. They would take him captive, and then he would be of no use to Melody. He had to sneak up on them. Take them by surprise. If he could get to Theo, he could stop the proceedings.

He crept into the cavern and hid behind a huge sparkling crystal column. This chamber was like a king's palace. Incredible shimmering stones lined the floor, ceiling, and walls. In the middle of the castle-like formations was an altar, and on it stood Melody.

The black cape she wore dwarfed her, as did the giant headpiece. Her painted white skin made her eyes so blue they looked like sapphires. A vampire untied Melody's cape, and it fell in a puddle around her feet. Next, the vampire removed the giant headdress, and Melody's glorious golden curls tumbled over her shoulders. With her lily-white skin, vivid blue eyes, and bright red lips, she looked like a porcelain doll.

He wanted desperately to wrap her in his arms and ease her fear, but he couldn't do that. He needed a plan—a way to free her from

Theo and his vampire clan. And he didn't have one yet.

Theo stood beside Melody, wearing a military-style overcoat decorated with patches of ancient Romanian characters. Theo slipped off the coat, exposing his bare chest. His torso was bandaged with a sash tied in an X. Tight black pants accentuated his muscular thighs. A blond curl fell over his forehead, giving his face a deceptively boyish quality.

Theo took hold of Melody's arm and pulled her toward him. "Now you are mine." He opened his mouth to expose his fangs and dipped his head, biting the side of her neck.

Blood spurted onto her chest and into her gold hair. Her screams echoed through the cave. A vein in Guystof's temple throbbed, and common sense vanished. He lunged forward, grabbing Theo around the waist. He was able to pull him away from Melody before Theo's vampires tackled him to the ground. He struggled against them, but it was useless. They had his arms and legs pinned.

Theo stood over him. "You're a bloody fool, brother. I didn't want to have to hurt you, but you refuse to give up even when it's obvious the game is over and I've won."

"Not as long as I'm still alive you haven't."

Theo laughed. "Don't be so melodramatic. I won't kill you, but I will keep you from ruining my plans." He snapped his fingers, and the vampires pulled Guystof up off the floor, keeping a strong hold on him, however. Theo walked over to Melody and touched her neck where the blood had started to dry.

"Don't touch me. I despise you."

"Ah, such a shame, my dear, since you'll be spending the next thousand years with me. Perhaps over time your feelings will change."

"Never," she cried out and slapped him hard across the face. Theo didn't flinch, but his eyes burned with fury, and Guystof knew that Melody had made a horrible mistake.

Theo grabbed her shoulders. "I was going to make this easy on you, but since you insist on fighting me, you will suffer the consequences." He leaned over and plunged his fangs into her neck like a pitchfork, sending blood spraying.

"Stop," Guystof screamed. "That's torture."

Theo pulled back from Melody's neck, blood dripping down his chin. "How does it feel to be under my control, brother? To know that soon your Melody will be my bride? You'll never again feel her lips on yours or hear her lovingly call your name."

Guystof struggled against the guards. "You'll never get away with this."

Theo chuckled. "But I already have. Soon Melody will be one of us, and then I will make her my wife, and there's nothing you can do about it."

"When Father learns of this—"

"Father," Theo spat. "I'm not afraid of him. Besides, what can he do? Disown me? I think not, for I shall be the one with the rich wife, while you will have nothing. You'll be the one disinherited. Face it. Game's over."

"Not by a long shot."

"I beg to differ. I'm a free man, and you, well, you're my prisoner." His laugh echoed throughout the chamber. "And I've had enough of you for one day. Ladies, indulge yourselves."

The female vampires were all over Guystof like vultures. There wasn't a part of him that didn't hurt from their feeding, but despite his torture, all he could think about was Melody. Her life was slipping away, and he was helpless to save her.

৪৩

"Please…don't hurt Guy." Melody's words were barely audible.

"I'd be more concerned with yourself." Theo stroked her head.

"I would have made this easier on you if you hadn't fought me. I do care about you, you know."

"Then let...me go."

"Now, you know I can't do that. You are going to die, my dear, but have no fear. It's only temporary. When you awaken, you'll be one of us."

"I don't want to...be like you."

Theo tapped his finger against her lips. "I'm surprised to hear you say that. You were more than willing to become a vampire when you agreed to marry my brother."

She opened her mouth to speak, but he clamped his hand over it. "Don't sap your strength. I know what you were going to say. You love Guystof. Well, I don't care, and I certainly don't want or need your love. And you shall never have mine. All you can expect or hope for is my companionship, and you will need it, my dear, if you hope to survive. There will be assassins who will want to hunt you down. Without me, you won't stand a chance."

Melody felt lightheaded and was having difficulty concentrating. She started to sink to the ground, but Theo held her up by the elbows.

"Just go with it. Don't fight it," he advised.

Although she would love to succumb to the grogginess—it would be easy to close her eyes and slip into darkness—she refused to give in.

"It's almost over, my dear," he whispered.

She cringed at the feeling of his hot breath on her ear and then felt the pressure to her neck as he once again helped himself to her blood. Her eyelids felt like lead. She fought to keep them open, but sleep was winning. Despite her efforts, her eyes closed, and the faces of her loved ones flashed before her—Mom and Dad, Ann, Mags, Billy, Gizmo, and her beloved Guy—then unable to hold on any longer, she surrendered to death.

℘ℭ

Melody's head lolled onto Theo's shoulder. Her lifeless body collapsed in his arms. The female vampires stepped back from Guystof, but Gelda kept her fangs in his neck.

"That's enough! Haven't you had your fill?" Theo yelled.

She looked up at him with blood dripping from her mouth. "Yes, of course. I'm sorry."

"Then come with me, and help get Melody settled. I want her to be comfortable when she wakes. The rest of you, take my brother to his room. When he comes to, Melody and I will be married, and he'll no longer be heir to Dragesa."

Theo scooped Melody up into his arms and carried her to a private chamber, where he laid her down gently on the bed, then covered her with a blanket. Although she would come to love the cold, it would take a while. He ran his hand across her cheek. Her skin was as soft as a rose petal. He was going to enjoy having her as a mate. He closed his eyes and imagined her beneath him, her smooth legs wrapped around his hips as he entered her. Oh yes, he was going to enjoy having her as his wife.

"Theo?"

Gelda's voice roused him from his daydream. He turned to her. "What is it?"

"Shall I tend to her wounds?" Gelda knelt by the side of the bed and held a cloth soaked in herbs that would help with the healing.

"Thank you. When you're finished, join me in my chambers. Unless, of course, you're too full from dinner to have dessert."

She smiled at him. "I'm never too full for you."

"Good answer." He brushed his lips over the side of her neck. "Don't keep me waiting. You know how impatient I am."

Theo left the room exhausted. Melody and Guystof had certainly

170

made the turning ceremony more exciting than most. What he needed now was to nap so he'd be well rested for his wedding. When he entered his chamber, he removed his coat and the sash from his waist, then collapsed on the bed. He closed his eyes and within seconds fell asleep.

After what seemed like only minutes, he was awakened by a crushing weight on his chest. Gelda was sprawled out on top of him. Naked. What a vision! Not soft and delicate like Melody. Lean and muscular. "Ah, you are anxious for me."

"Of course, as I always am." She smiled, and the glint of pearly fangs peeked through her gum-line.

He kissed her hard. Her fang broke the skin on his lip, and he tasted blood. He pushed her back from him and smiled as he ran his hands over her breasts, across her flat stomach, then down along her hips.

She squealed and wriggled on top of him. His desire for her grew hot and hard, and he unzipped his pants, sinking his manhood deep into her. She cried out, then bit the side of his neck as he thrust into her again and again.

When he could stand it no longer, he curled his lip back and bit her just above the shoulder blade. Blood filled his mouth and trickled down his throat. Soon his hunger began to subside, and he took pleasure in their rhythm.

Later, when he lay spent, he found himself thinking about Melody. He turned his wrist and looked at his watch. 3:00 A.M. Melody would be waking soon.

He rolled Gelda off him, then turned on his side, his head propped by his hand. "You were fabulous." He touched the tip of her nose with his finger.

"So were you." She planted a soft kiss on his chest. "That mortal woman will never service you as I do." Her voice dripped venom, and her emerald eyes flashed.

He leaned over her and cupped his hand around her long, slender throat. "Do I detect jealousy?" She struggled as his fingers pressed against her windpipe.

"Stop!" She choked, grabbing at his hand. "I'm sorry."

He pressed a bit harder.

"Yes. I'm jealous," she rasped.

He kissed her cheek and released his hold. "No need to be. You'll always be my favorite."

"But you're going to marry her." Gelda's voice came out as a croak.

Theo took hold of her hand and rubbed his thumb over it. "It's a marriage of convenience, that's all. You know that. And speaking of my marriage, I need to get dressed, and you need to go ready my bride."

Gelda left his bed, clearly not happy. Her full lips were turned down and a frown line marred the usually smooth skin between her brows. She scooped her cape up off the floor and flung it over her shoulders, nearly knocking a candle from his bedside table.

Theo stood. He took hold of her arm and swung her to him, kissing her passionately. "Make Melody beautiful for me," he murmured against her lips.

She smiled slyly. "Ah, you can be sure of that, but not as beautiful as me." She strode from the room, tall and proud, her hips swinging seductively.

Theo knew she was aware that he watched her. She was full of fire and the only vampire that he'd let get away with having that sharp tongue.

He took a long, leisurely shower, then put on black pants and a white dress shirt. He studied his appearance in the gilt-framed wall mirror as he combed his hair. He was handsome. There was no doubt of that. Women adored him. There was no denying that either. Except Melody. She despised him. A slight smile curved his full mouth. He loved a challenge. He would enjoy changing her mind. She might never love him as Gelda did, but she would grow to care for him. He was sure of that. When he wanted to, he could charm a woman so that she found him irresistible.

A knock sounded on his door. He set his comb down and strode across the room. When he swung the door open, he was surprised to find Gelda back so soon. Her pale skin looked whiter than usual, and her emerald eyes were dark with worry.

"Come quick. Something's wrong with your brother."

CHAPTER THIRTEEN

Guystof lay motionless on the bed. Theo touched his brother's forehead. It was ice cold. He turned Guystof's wrist over and felt for a pulse. There wasn't one. "How could this have happened?"

Gelda twisted her hands in the folds of her cape. "I don't know. I came to check on him...to make sure he'd been put in the correct bedchamber—you know how your guards can be careless at times— and found him like this. I've never know any vampire to be so cold."

"That's because he's dead." Theo's words cut through the air like a sword.

"No, no. Don't say that." She stepped forward and rubbed Guystof's hands between her own. "He'll wake. You'll see."

Theo pushed Gelda away, and his brother's arm hung limply over the side of the bed. "This is your fault. You did this." Fury boiled his blood.

She stared at him, her eyes wide with shock. "I-I don't know what you mean. I did everything you asked of me."

"I let you drink from him. And what did you do? You drained him dry. Took too much of his blood with your greed."

Gelda's back visibly stiffened. Her green eyes turned black with fear. "No, that's not true. I drank no more than the others. How can you blame me? This wouldn't have happened if you hadn't instructed us to feed on him."

"Are you blaming me?" His voice echoed through the chamber.

Gelda backed up and cowered against the wall. "No, no. Of c-course not. I'm just s-saying it was no one's fault. An accident."

"An accident?" He looked down at his brother's handsome features. A part of him truly cared for Guystof. A memory of when they were boys sprang to mind. They had hunted together back then, and his brother had been his protector. Looking out for him had been Guystof's passion. His mother's death had affected him deeply. He blamed himself for not being able to save her and made sure his younger brother would not meet the same fate. Theo's eyelids grew hot. He took a deep breath and quickly pushed the memories of his youth from his mind. No use getting sentimental. Nothing would change what had happened.

"I suppose it will serve no purpose to cast blame now. That won't bring him back." He sat on the bed and rested his head in his hands. "But we have to deal with the consequences of his death. Father will be furious, and all my dreams of ruling Dragesa will be lost."

Gelda came forward and placed her hand on his shoulder. "Don't worry. You'll come up with something. You always do."

"Ah, but this time is different. I've gone too far. I'm responsible for the death of my own flesh and blood."

"No one need know."

"And how do you suggest I pull that off? It's not as if my brother won't be missed."

"Guystof's death doesn't have to be blamed on you. Your father doesn't know about any of this. Not about the caves. Not about your plot to steal Melody. Not about what happened last night. And he doesn't have to know…ever. This can be our secret."

"But Father will investigate Guystof's death. It's not common to find a vampire dead in his bed…"

"Not if there's no mystery as to how he died."

Theo narrowed his eyes as he tried to follow her train of thought.

"What if we staged it to look like your brother turned Melody into a vampire, and in her naïveté, she fed too long on him?"

"My dear brother killed by his beloved in a wild night of passion." Theo thought hard about that, then sat up with a sly smile curving the corners of his mouth. "And poor Melody, a young vampire, vulnerable and alone. She'll need a protector. And who better than the new heir to Dragesa." He took hold of Gelda's hand and kissed it. "You're a very clever woman. I can have my wedding out in the open now, not in the cave's shadows. And I will have Father's best wishes."

Gelda pulled her hand away from his. "You still want to marry her?"

"It's not a matter of want. It's out of necessity. I need her money for Dragesa." He stood and pulled Gelda into his arms. "Melody means nothing to me. We need to hurry, though, and get her before she wakes."

They traveled through the castle's passageways, taking care not to be seen. Only when they reached the caves did Theo relax a little. He would remain on edge until this task had been fully executed. Luckily, they found Melody still asleep and it was without much trouble that they were able to deliver her to Guystof's bedchamber and position her in bed beside him.

Theo scrutinized the scene. Melody's painted skin, fishnet tights, corset, and petticoat were not his brother's style. If he wanted to set this up to be believable, he would have to change Melody's appearance. She needed some suitable sleepwear, and there wasn't time to rummage through her room. There was only one way for him to fix that. The old-fashioned way. With magic. He closed his eyes and moved his hands over Melody's body, envisioning her skin a pale ivory and her wearing a lacy, rose-colored nightgown. Guystof was a sucker for frills. He opened his eyes at Gelda's startled gasp.

"Oh, Theo. That's perfect. Melody looks like herself again."

He smiled. "But we're not finished yet. We have to deal with my brother now."

"I don't understand. What more needs to be done?"

Theo pointed to Guystof. "Look at him. He needs to look disheveled after his wild night with Melody. Mess up his hair."

Gelda did as instructed. "How's that?"

Theo studied the bed scene a little longer. They'd missed the most important details. "Guystof's wounds have healed. We need fresh marks on his neck and blood on the sheet if this is to be truly believable."

"It's a good thing you're so clever.'

"Well, what are you waiting for?"

Her jaw dropped open. "You have to be kidding. You want me to bite him?"

Theo nodded. "Is that a problem?"

Gelda looked at Guystof's still body and grimaced. "That's disgusting. He's dead."

"But it needs to be done." Without giving it another thought, Theo leaned over his brother, then curled back his front lip and let his fangs protrude. He pierced two perfect holes in the side of Guystof's neck. Soon the white pillowcase was stained red. Theo wiped his mouth on his shirtsleeve. The blood tasted bitter in death. "What do you think of this picture now?"

Gelda stepped closer to the bed. "It's perfect."

Melody would be in for a shock when she woke, finding her beloved dead beside her. She'd have no memory of the turning ceremony. New vampires never did. What she would have would be an almost insatiable appetite for blood. There was no doubt Melody would think she was responsible for Guystof's death.

Theo chuckled softly, quite pleased with his work. However, he couldn't stand there forever admiring it. He couldn't run the risk that his father might still be suspicious. All evidence of his secret haven below the castle had to be erased.

They returned to the caves, and he closed his eyes to visualize the caverns the way they were before he'd inhabited them—pristine. He waited a few moments, then opened his eyes and all signs of occupancy had been erased. Only his vampires, roosting high in the ceiling, remained.

He called to them. His voice bounced off the flowstone walls. Each one lined up before him. "It's no longer safe here. You all must leave."

Gelda's eyes were wide with surprise. "Even me?"

Theo placed his arm over her shoulders and pulled her to him. He kissed the side of her neck, then ran his mouth over her ear. "I'm sorry, but yes. It's not safe for you here."

The color drained from her face. "I don't care. I'm not afraid. Not as long as I'm with you."

"That's very courageous, my dear, but you still need to go." Theo kissed her hard, then held her out at arms' length and studied her. He wanted to remember every curve of her body, the sparkle in her emerald eyes, and the way her lips curved up at the corners even when she wasn't smiling. She was beautiful, loyal, and his, yet he had no idea when he might see her again.

"Then come with me," she pleaded.

"I can't. I have to stay at Dragesa."

"But I can make you happy. We can travel the world together. Home is where you make it."

"Ah, sounds lovely, my dear, but I only have one home. It's right here; and I will not give it up unless I am forced to. The game is not quite over yet."

She turned her head away and stared at the floor.

"This is not good-bye," he whispered. "I will find you no matter where you are and bring you back here when it is safe."

She looked up at him, a hopeful gleam in her eyes. "Promise?"

He kissed her tenderly. "I promise."

ൠ

Melody rolled onto her back. She felt like he'd been hit by a truck. Every bone in her body ached. Her blurred vision took in her surroundings. Where the devil was she? In a bedchamber, but whose? She turned her head to the side and gasped. Guy! She was in Guy's bed?

She squeezed her eyes shut. What had happened? The last thing she remembered... Well, she didn't know what she remembered. Everything was fuzzy.

She stroked the side of his cheek. It was cold. Very cold. She put her hand over his. It too was cold. She sat up and took hold of his shoulders. She shook them gently at first, then, when he didn't respond, she shook harder. "Guy! Wake up! What's wrong with you?"

Though his features were relaxed as if in sleep, his white skin and pale blue lips told a different story. And a pool of red covered the sheet beneath him.

Her chest tightened, and she felt the air being sucked from her lungs. No, no, no. It couldn't be true. Her beloved Guy couldn't be dead. How could he? It wasn't until she saw the trickle of dried blood from the two perfect holes piercing his neck that she had a suspicion of what had happened. Her stomach rumbled with hunger and saliva filled her mouth. She ran her tongue along her swollen gums and felt the prick of fangs. She was a vampire!

She ran her lips over Guy's cold cheek, then covered his mouth with her own and tried to breathe life back into him. But he was cold, oh so cold. Had she done this to him? Had she somehow killed him? She scrunched her eyes shut, trying to remember how that could have happened.

A knock sounded on the door, rousing her from her misery. She opened her eyes.

"Master?"

It was Blakesley's voice.

The door opened slowly, and the old butler peeked in. When he saw them on the bed, he appeared embarrassed; then a wide smile lit his withered features. "So sorry to interrupt, sir, but I've been so worried about you and Miss Melody. I was just about to go to your father, when I thought it best to check your room first."

"He's dead," Melody cried.

Blakesley put a hand over his mouth in horror. He swayed, then reached for the doorframe to steady himself. "That's not possible. Not Master Guystof. I told him it wasn't safe to go after you alone. But he's so stubborn. Wouldn't listen to my warning." He crossed the room to study Guy. "Theo is capable of just about anything, but I never thought he would kill his own brother."

Melody stared at Blakesley in disbelief. "Theo? He did this?"

"You don't remember?"

She shook her head. "Remember what?"

"Oh my! Theo kidnapped you and took you down into the caves beneath the castle. He was going to marry you. Master Guystof found out and went down into the caves after you, but Theo must have caught him and…"

Tears ran down her cheeks. "You mean I didn't do this?"

"Why, how could you have thought so?"

"I don't know. I don't know what to think. My head is pounding, and everything is a blur." She balled her hands into fists and rubbed furiously at her eyes. "The last thing I remember is opening the door to my room, thinking it was my luggage, but it was Theo." Her voice rose in pitch. "Everything after that is blank...until now. I woke and found Guy dead." She opened her mouth and exposed her new fangs. "I'm a vampire."

Blakesley backed toward the door. "Miss, calm down. It's probably best that you don't remember." He didn't take his eyes off her face. "Your skin is becoming gray and your pupils yellow. You must need to feed."

Melody stared at him in horror. "What do I do?" Her voice came out as little more than a croak now.

"You'll need to hunt for your food, or find someone you can feed on." Blakesley was nearly at the door, and she could see that his hands were shaking.

"Please, don't leave. I promise I won't hurt you."

"Maybe not intentionally, Miss Melody, but as a newly turned vampire, you'll not be able to control your urges."

"But you can't leave me alone. What will I do? And what about Guy? I can't just leave him here." Panic started to take hold of her, and she felt all reason slipping away. Her hunger was growing, and the saliva in her mouth burned her tongue. She didn't want to hurt Blakesley, but if something didn't happen quickly, she might not be able to control herself. "Please, help me."

He shifted his gaze away from her and back to Guy. "You're right. I must do something. If you were to take the potion I gave to Master Guystof, it should keep you from needing to feed. Once we've taken care of that problem, then we can think about what to do next."

"Oh, thank you."

"It shouldn't take long for me to get it."

After Blakesley left, she walked over to the window and stared out at the night sky. Stars twinkled, and the Southern Cross stood out like a beacon. Not so long ago, she and Guy had looked at it together. Now he was gone. And they'd never do anything together again. She crossed her arms over her chest and rocked back and forth. How could she go on without him?

Through tear blurred eyes, she glanced over at his still figure on the bed and was overcome with grief. When Blakesley returned, she had no way of knowing whether he'd been gone a minute or an hour, nor did she care. Her body and mind were numb.

Blakesley dropped a leather-bound ledger on the table and opened a vial of potion. "One drop is all you need."

She wiped the tears from her cheeks before taking the vial from him. "Do you think it will make me sick?"

He looked at her with surprise. "What makes you ask that?"

"Guy kept getting pains in his stomach. He assumed they were due to the potion."

Blakesley sat on a chair next to the table. "How much potion was he taking daily? Do you know?"

"I think he said he'd gotten up to five or six drops."

Blakesley grimaced. "No wonder he'd been sick. He was supposed to take only one."

Melody tilted her head back, poured a drop of the amber liquid onto her tongue, and swallowed.

Blakesley flipped through the ledger. "Do you remember when the pains started?"

Her brow furrowed. "Right after we met."

"Really? That's interesting. Ambrus, Master Guystof's

grandfather, created the potion, hoping to break the spell put on the kingdom by Lazlo, an evil sorcerer. He'd been taking it for years, gradually increasing the dosage. But he was never able to retain his human form for any length of time. When Lazlo discovered Ambrus had been conducting experiments, he threatened to kill his family, but Ambrus traded his life for theirs. That was when he began to get pains in his stomach. I remember that time vividly. And besides, Ambrus recorded it right here." Blakesley placed his finger near the bottom of the page.

Melody leaned over his shoulder and read. "He thought the potion was poisoning him."

"But what if the potion had nothing to do with the pain?"

Melody looked up at him. "Then what do you think caused it?"

Blakesley slammed the ledger shut. "Love. Ambrus loved Berta and Cato more than anything in the world. The way that Master Guystof loved you. I think the more he was falling in love with you, the more human he was becoming. And that was making him sick. The vampire in him was fighting the transformation."

"So the combination of the potion and unconditional love could be the recipe needed to remove the curse." Melody lifted the bottle back to her mouth, but Blakesley held her arm.

"Wait! We don't know what too much of the potion might do to you. This is only a theory. What if Ambrus was right? It might very well poison you."

"That's a risk I'm willing to take. If I can lift the curse, then maybe, just maybe, I can bring Guy back too."

"And if you're wrong, it might kill you."

❧❧

Theo stood in stunned disbelief at the state of his chambers. Broken vials littered the floor. Potion splattered his walls. His gray metal cabinet was open. His magic goblet was on his desk, filled with blood. He had no doubt who'd done this. Guystof. But he couldn't have acted alone. That sneaky Blakesley was the only one who could possibly have gotten hold of Theo's keys. What else had he done? Did that prying butler know of the caves? And of Melody's kidnapping? Theo lifted his magic chalice and flung it against the wall. Blood sprayed everywhere, and the goblet crashed to the floor with a thud.

"Damn him!" Blakesley might know everything. He might have already gone to Father. Things were not going at all as he'd planned. *Think. Think.* There had to be a way out of this. He walked over to the window. Hundreds of bats streamed across the sky like a giant black cloud. His vampires were leaving. If only he hadn't sent Gelda away. She'd know what to do. He remembered her words. *"Home is where you make it."* He could live anywhere in the world. Besides, it would only be temporary. Eventually, he'd be forgiven, and then he could return to Dragesa. In the meantime, there were plenty of lovely young women he could seduce. Theo closed his eyes and imagined where he'd like to go.

CHAPTER FOURTEEN

Melody drank the entire bottle of potion, gagging a few times at its bitter taste. As she waited for what she hoped would be a reversal of the curse, needle-like pains shot through her insides, and she doubled over in agony.

"Oh, Miss Melody," Blakesley cried, draping his arm around her and ushering her over to a chair. "I was afraid this would happen. Too much of the potion is dangerous. I just hope it doesn't kill you."

She leaned back against the worn velvet cushions and closed her eyes, grimacing as another wave of pain ripped through her. Beads of perspiration on her forehead rolled down the sides of her face.

"I'll fetch you a cool cloth," Blakesley said.

Before he could go, Melody grabbed hold of his arm. "No, stay. I-I don't want to be alone." Her voice was barely above a whisper, but she had no doubt that he'd heard her, for her eyes, open now, were fixated on his face.

Concern had etched more lines into his skin, and the corners of his mouth were tipped down in a frown. However, he nodded agreement to her request, then took her hand in his and squeezed. "You're a strong woman, Miss Melody."

A faint smile cracked her lips, but then a second later, she gritted her teeth as the pain intensified and all rational thought left her. Through her delirium, she heard a woman screaming. It wasn't until Blakesley took her by the shoulders and shook her that she realized she had been that woman. "Maybe I'm not so strong after all," she panted.

"Just hang on. Hang on," he begged.

"I'm trying." She gripped the edge of the chair. A searing heat raged from the tips of her toes all the way up to her scalp. "What's happening to me?"

"I don't know." Blakesley grabbed hold of her legs and put his full weight on them as she began to kick wildly at the air. "But your skin is darkening like you've spent an entire summer in the sun."

"What? Even on Fiji, I barely got a decent tan."

"Well, you're positively glowing."

Just as Blakesley uttered those words, the burning sensation was replaced with itching. It started on the palms of her hands and traveled throughout her entire body, growing more intense with each second. She scratched at her arms, neck and chest like a dog infested with fleas, and then her fangs broke through her gum line, and she gnawed her skin raw.

A giant welt appeared on her wrist, itching worse than a hundred mosquito bites. When she sank her fangs into her own flesh, she thought the potion must have made her insane. But she didn't care. All she wanted was for this nightmare to end.

Blood spurted from her arm and dripped from her mouth. Blakesley let go of her, his eyes wide with fear. As he backed away, she pleaded, "Don't go. Please. I won't hurt you. I promise."

"I don't know what more I can do to help you." He inched toward the door, never shifting his gaze off her face.

"Just don't leave me." Tears blurred her vision as she watched him go.

However, before he reached the door, he stopped. "Miss Melody, your fangs, they're gone!"

She ran her tongue across her teeth. He was right. She couldn't feel them under her gum line either. The itching had gone away too. And so had her insatiable appetite. "It worked. The curse is lifted. I'm no longer a vampire."

She sprang out of the chair, raced over to Blakesley, and hugged him. "Doesn't it feel wonderful to be human again?" When he didn't answer, she pulled back from him and saw fangs. "You're still a vampire? It only worked on me?"

He nodded and pushed her away. "Go on. You must leave here before I do something awful. I never feed on humans. I find it abhorrent. Animals—usually rabbits and squirrels—are what I eat. But with your blood so close…"

She looked down at the blood dripping from her wrist. "Then take the potion. If it worked on me, it should work on you. That's how we'll lift the curse. Each vampire will drink an entire bottle of potion."

A frown furrowed his brow. "If only we had more. But you drank the last of it. "

She held her wrist out to him. "Then go on. Feed on me. Just this once. Do it for me and Guy."

He looked at her in surprise. "I don't understand."

"The potion is in my blood. If you drink from me, my blood should work for you in the same magical way as the potion did for me."

"But if it doesn't and I drink too much, I could kill you."

"It's worth a try." She held her arm out in front of him as her blood dripped onto his shirt.

He hesitated a second, and then she felt a quick sharp prick as his fangs entered her skin, piercing deeper into the holes she'd made herself.

She had no idea how much blood would equal a bottle of potion, so she let him drink until she became dizzy, then waited for him to experience the same agony she had as he left his vampire body behind and was reborn as a human. But it didn't happen. Instead, astonishment touched his face.

"No pain." He ran his tongue over his gums. "And no fangs. I'm human. Miss Melody, you were right. Your blood is indeed magical and even better than the potion."

"Now I just hope it can bring Guy back." Melody sat on the edge of the bed and gently stroked his cheek. "Please come back to me."

Without further hesitation, she dripped the blood from her wrist into his mouth, then lifted his head, forcing it to trickle down his throat. She sat with him for a long time, letting her blood fill him, until a light-headed sensation washed over her and she knew she could give no more. She scanned the room for Blakesley and found him standing by the window, basking in the morning sunshine. "It feels good, doesn't it?"

He nodded, but looked at her with despair. "Your blood's not going to work for Master Guystof."

Melody swallowed the lump in her throat. She shifted her gaze back to Guy, so still and cold beside her, and couldn't stop the flow of tears running down her cheeks. No, it wasn't going to work for him. Perhaps he'd been dead too long. Whatever the reason, it didn't matter. All that did matter was that he wasn't coming back to her. Not now. Not ever. Sobs shook her body.

Blakesley came over to her and put his hand on her arm. "Miss Melody, there's nothing more you can do. Please, come with me. I'll get you something to help you relax."

"I need to say good-bye." She waited until he went back to stand by the window before pressing her cheek against Guy's and whispering, "I'll never love anyone the way I love you. Ever." Then she closed her eyes and kissed him. His lips warmed. His breath caressed her cheek, and she thought she must be dreaming.

She opened her eyes slowly. To her disbelief, Guy stirred, so she kissed him again, waking him fully.

A warm glow flowed through her as he looked at her lovingly. "Have I been asleep long?"

"Seems like forever."

"Sounds like you missed me."

"More than you'll ever know."

He stretched, then sat up and wrapped his arms around her. "What's that?" he asked, staring at the bottle on the bedside table. "Is that my potion?"

Melody shifted her gaze across the room to Blakesley, hoping for some help, but he merely shrugged and said, "I'm going outside to enjoy the sunshine. It's been hundreds of years since I've done that."

"What of the curse?" Guy asked.

"That's for the miss to tell you." Blakesley winked at Melody, then left the room with a spring in his step.

Guy took the vial from the table and tipped it over. No potion spilled out. "You drank it?" His voice was tinged with horror. "Do you have any idea how dangerous that was?"

Melody buried her face against his chest. "I'd do anything for you."

He drew her from him and looked directly into her eyes. "So when are you going to tell me what's been going on here?"

"It's a long story."

"There's no place I'd rather be than right here with you. So start talking."

She plucked at the bedspread. "What's the last thing you remember?"

His brow wrinkled, and a frown tightened his mouth. "Theo held you captive. He was going to turn you into a vampire. I tried to stop him, but he turned his minions on me." He stared hard at her. "Did he turn you?"

When she didn't answer right away, his eyes hardened. "He did, didn't he?"

More than a little nervous at what he might want to do to his brother, she said, "It doesn't matter now. That's all in the past."

"Past or not, it matters to me." He pulled her back into his arms. "What did he do to you?"

Melody rested her head against his shoulder. "I don't remember the turning ceremony. But when I woke up, I was in bed with you and…you were dead," she said reluctantly. "That's why I took the potion. To lift the curse and bring you back to me."

"I wasn't merely asleep; I was dead?"

"Yes."

"And you were a vampire." Guy's voice was low and guarded.

"Yes." She could feel his uneven breathing on her cheek and worried that he'd do something rash that could lead to more death. "Revenge isn't the answer. We should find Theo and his vampires so I can give them my blood, and then we can all live in peace."

"I don't understand. Why would you need to give them your blood?"

"Well, the potion didn't work exactly as I'd hoped. It removed the curse, but just from me, unless you drink my blood. Seems I'm magical."

"I always knew that," he whispered into her hair. "Enough about Theo. All I care about is you and our wedding."

Joy bubbled inside her. "Then we have lots to do. There's a menu to prepare, flowers to order, and invitations to write. Of course, I'll fly my family and friends here. Gizmo too." Her mind was awhirl. She was going to have a beautiful wedding in a magnificent castle.

Her daydream came to a screeching halt, though, as her gaze focused on the room's tattered drapes, worn bedspread, and old dark furniture. She might be getting married in a castle, but it was far from magnificent. It could be, though. She could bring it back to its original grandeur. After all, she had the fortune to do it. A wide smile spread across her face. "I hope you don't mind if I spruce up the castle."

He didn't return her smile. "You don't have to do that, Melody. I'm not marrying you for your money."

She wrapped her arms around him. "I know you're not. I want to do this. Besides, this is going to be my home too, and I want it to be perfect for both of us."

"There are so many reasons why I love you, and your thoughtfulness is right at the top of the list. I don't deserve you."

"We deserve each other," she said softly.

His lips brushed against hers, then he delivered a series of slow, shivery kisses.

₧₨

The next few weeks flew by. Guy's father welcomed her into the family as if she was already his daughter-in-law. She was able to show her appreciation by giving him and all the LeBreque servants her blood, releasing them from the curse. Only Theo and his harem were left as vampires, since their whereabouts were unknown. However, when they returned to Dragesa, she would do the same for them.

She'd hired a team of experts to redo the castle, and it now sparkled like a magnificent gem, making it the perfect place for her wedding. Her mom and dad, Ann, Mags, Billy, and Gizmo had flown in yesterday.

It was hard to believe she'd planned a wedding in such a short period of time, but it had come together without a hitch. They were going to be married later that afternoon in the Great Hall, with the people she loved most around her.

She sat on the edge of her bed with Gizmo on her lap. The little black pug licked her shower-moistened skin. Obviously, he'd missed her as much as she'd missed him. She looked down at her left hand and smiled. Guy had presented her with an engagement ring last night at dinner, and she'd never seen anything more beautiful. The square-cut, three-carat sapphire was surrounded by thirteen brilliant diamonds, but the best part was it had belonged to his mother.

She looked across the room at her wedding dress hanging over her closet door. The delicate lace gown was strapless and slim fitting with a slightly scooped neckline, ruched waistband, and Swarovski crystals. It was absolutely breathtaking and exactly what she'd always dreamed of wearing.

Melody nudged Gizmo off her lap and padded over to her dressing table. She was combing through her wet hair when a knock sounded at her door.

"Mel, may I come in?"

Guy? She set the comb down and quickly draped a garment bag over her wedding dress. "Yes, but what are you doing here? You should be getting ready."

When she opened the door, her stomach fluttered. Though handsome as always, he was wearing khakis and a polo shirt. Hardly wedding attire. "You're not having second thoughts about marrying me, are you?" she asked nervously.

He pulled her into his arms and kissed her. "Did that reassure you?" There was a twinkle in his eyes.

"A little."

"Just a little?" He slipped her robe off her shoulder and covered her skin with kisses, starting at the top of her breasts, moving to the base of her neck, and then up to her lips.

She was left breathless and tingling with desire. If things went any further, they'd miss their own wedding. "I'm sure now," she said against his cheek.

"Good. But actually, I came here to ask you the very same thing. Are you sure you want to live here in Moldavia and help me rule Dragesa?" He took a document stamped with the royal seal from his pocket and held it out for her to read.

Her eyes grew wide as she took in its meaning. "Your father turned over the kingdom to you."

"It's a huge responsibility, but there's no one I'd rather share it with than you."

Her body grew hot, and her hands began to sweat. Could she handle that? Meek little Melody from Hope? But as she looked into his magnetic blue eyes, she realized that girl was gone and in her place was a strong, self-assured woman.

She wrapped her arms around his neck, bringing his mouth down to hers and leaving him with no question as to her answer.

"Don't worry," he beamed. "I'll be dressed and ready in no time and waiting for you at the altar."

Right after he left, there was another knock at her door. "What did you forget to ask this time?" She laughed.

Before she crossed the room, the door burst open. The first thing she spotted was the halo of copper curls; next was the skintight miniskirt, then the four-inch heels. "Sugar!"

The hairdresser sashayed across the floor, deposited her train case on a chair, and enveloped Melody in a bear hug. "It's so great to see you, hon."

"I'm so glad you're here, but how—"

"That man of yours arranged for me to come. Can't have you doing your own hair and makeup on such an important day when you can have an artiste do it for you." Sugar giggled. "Well, come on, time's a wasting. We can talk and catch up as we work."

Melody sat down at her dressing table. Sugar worked her magic while Melody chatted on and on about Guy. Before long, her hair and makeup were done. All she needed to do now was step into her gown.

When she looked in the mirror, she couldn't believe her eyes. She looked every bit the countess she would soon become.

Sugar handed her the bouquet, and there were tears in her eyes. "Oh, Mel, you're having the fairy-tale wedding every girl dreams of."

Melody smiled. It hadn't all happened quite like she'd planned, but the ending was perfect.

She left her bedroom and walked to the top of the staircase. Her father stood below, waiting to escort her to the ceremony. As she started down the stairs, she realized her hands were shaking. When she reached the bottom step, her father offered her his arm.

"Are you ready?" he asked.

She took a deep breath and nodded.

As they walked together past all the people who loved her, there was only one face she focused on—the handsome man with the ice-blue eyes—and the way he looked at her made her blush.

She had to be the luckiest girl in the world. First, she won the lottery, then she found her soul mate on a reality show. She was proof that dreams really do come true.

EPILOGUE

The strobe lights pulsated with the beat of the music. The glass dance floor changed color every few minutes, illuminating the bodies twisting and turning so they looked like giant fireflies. Theo watched a pretty brunette in a silver miniskirt dance seductively. She had gorgeous legs. As if aware he was watching, she hiked her skirt up a little bit higher and winked at him. Theo smiled and waggled his finger at her, then patted the barstool beside him.

"Hey, handsome. What're you drinking?" A blond with big blue eyes sat down on the other side of him. She flipped her straight hair over one shoulder, exposing a long, slender neck.

"Bloody Mary." He flashed her his most charming smile.

Monte Carlo was ripe with young, single women. Rich women. He could get used to this.

The bartender set a drink down in front of him. He stirred it slowly while he ran his hand over her thigh. "Are you from around here?"

She laughed. "No, I just come here to party."

"So you like to have fun?" He moved his hand over her silky smooth skin.

"Of course." She inched closer to him on the stool.

"I'm not interrupting, am I?" The brunette from the dance floor sat beside him.

"No. We were just talking about having fun." He placed his other hand on her leg, moving his fingers up under her miniskirt. "Care to join us?"

"I'm always up for a good time." She crossed her legs, closing Theo's hand between her warm thighs.

A rush of cool breath caressed the back of his neck, then he felt lips glide over his skin.

"I leave you for a few minutes, and you've already replaced me."

The husky voice fell like music across his ears. Strands of red hair tickled his cheek.

He spun the stool around so that he faced her.

Gelda's emerald eyes twinkled playfully.

"My dear, no one could ever replace you." He twirled the girls' stools so that they too faced her. "These are my new friends, and they're looking to have a good time tonight."

"How lucky for them to have found us." She smiled sweetly at them. "We have all the time in the world to play."

Theo ran his tongue across his front teeth, feeling the prick of his fangs break his gum line. "That we do, love. That we do."

Also by Raine English

The Romance Reborn Series

Book One

TIN ANGEL

For the first time in Alice Hart's life, she likes the way she looks. The ugly duckling has become a swan. But how could this be? She's ninety years old, far from young and beautiful...

Alice Hart is a lonely old woman who believes true love happens only once in a lifetime. When the angel Christmas tree topper given to her by the fiancé she lost sixty years ago comes to life, Alice's wish to be young again is granted, but she's given only ten days to find true love or die unfulfilled. So she concocts a story that she's Alice's long lost niece, hoping to attract the attention of the handsome tenant renting her upstairs apartment.

Disillusioned by his experiences with high-maintenance women, Jack Billings yearns to find an old-fashioned girl who is more interested in his heart than in material things. When his elderly landlady vanishes, her newly arrived niece, Ally, seems to hold the clues to her disappearance. Jack at first dismisses Ally as another material girl, but as he digs deeper into Alice's mystery, he learns that Ally is more than what she seems and worries that the girl he's coming to love might be a scam artist or worse.

Please enjoy the following excerpt for *TIN ANGEL*...

CHAPTER ONE

"*H*ow's this look?"

Alice Hart leaned forward in the overstuffed armchair, squinting her tired eyes to get a better look at the tin angel Jack Billings had set atop the Christmas tree. Wrapped with faded gold foil and netting, the angel was almost as old as she.

"The tree looks wonderful, Jack. Whatever would I do without you?" She smiled at the handsome young man who'd come to her rescue countless times over the five months he'd been renting her upstairs apartment. A tumble of black hair fell across the bluest eyes she'd ever seen. He brushed it back and flashed her a Cary Grant grin.

"Aw, you're such a charmer, you'd have no trouble rounding up one of your other admirers." He stepped down off the stool and stood next to her chair.

Alice swooshed a wrinkled, liver-spotted hand through the air. "Go on, it's Saturday night. You mustn't waste your time with an old woman. Go on, before you're late for your date."

Jack's deep, throaty laughter filled the parlor. Alice liked the sound of it. She didn't get many visitors. Pastor Riley and Doc

Brooks didn't count. They came weekly out of obligation, but Jack came because he wanted to. She tucked the wool blanket on her lap snugly around her legs. If only she were young again, she just might pursue a man like Jack.

"What makes you think I have a date?" He got down on one knee and rested an elbow on the arm of her chair. With his chin in his hand, he stared deeply into her eyes. "There's no one I'd rather be with than you," he teased, but there was a kindness in his voice that touched her.

"Careful or you'll make me blush." She plucked at the blanket with long, spindly fingers—fingers that had once been beautiful and able to fly gracefully over ivory piano keys. But that was years ago, before the arthritis had set in. "The tree looks beautiful," she said, shifting her gaze.

"Beautiful, indeed. I'll be back tomorrow to check on you." He leaned over and gently kissed her cheek.

His finely sculpted lips were warm. A tingle ran down her spine, burning a trail of shame. She was ninety years old. She shouldn't still have these feelings. Yet she realized that was one of old age's cruelest tricks. While on the outside she had grayed and withered, inside she still felt twenty-five.

Alice squeezed his large, strong hands and bid him good night. After Jack left, she leaned back in the chair and stared at the Christmas tree. The glass ornaments twinkled against the multicolored lights. A deep, hollow feeling filled her chest. This could very well be her last Christmas. At her age, how many more could she expect to have? Tears pricked at her lids. She never imagined her life would turn out as it had, but then does anyone ever imagine they'll wind up alone? Even now, after more than sixty years, she could still picture Thomas Long's face—his lopsided smile that sent her heart pitter-pattering every time he flashed it her way, and those deep chocolate eyes that looked straight into her soul.

A tear trickled down her cheek. The war had taken Tom before they could marry. But he wasn't the only one who'd died that awful day in 1942. She'd died along with him. At least in spirit. If it hadn't been for Hart Theater, the family business where she played the piano each night, she'd have had no reason to ever leave her parents' rambling Victorian home.

Jasper, a sleek black cat with piercing gold eyes, jumped onto her lap. He curled into a ball and let out a raspy, contented purr. "At least I've got you," Alice whispered, stroking his back.

She shouldn't have let life slip by. Surely there could've been someone, somewhere who'd have found her attractive. If only she'd put herself out in the world, perhaps she'd have met someone…someone like Jack. He was just the type of man she would love to have met when she was young. The kind of man Tom had been—gentle and considerate. A lump formed in her throat. Nothing about life was fair.

She stared past the gleaming Christmas tree, through the leaded glass windows, out to the snow-lined street. She'd lived in Silvercreek her entire life. She'd watched the small Connecticut farming community become a bustling industrial town, but she'd never truly been a part of it—just a bystander looking in from the outside. She sighed and closed her eyes. What she wouldn't give to be able to live life over, if only for a few weeks. To be twenty-five again and in love…

Something sharp scratched Alice's arm. She opened her heavy-lidded eyes to find Jasper stretching contentedly on her lap. The grandfather clock ticking softly in the room's shadowed corner showed midnight. She'd fallen asleep in the parlor again. She pushed out her bottom lip and shook her head sadly. Pretty soon she'd be sleeping through the night in the chair.

Nudging the cat off her lap, Alice reached for her cane. Even with support, her legs were wobbly, and her joints ached from rheumatism. Slowly, she made her way to the bedroom. She slipped into a nightgown and then took the hairpins from the bun at the top of her head. Long silver strands cascaded down her back, falling just below her waist. She'd always worn her hair long, even as a child. It covered her like a blanket, hiding her imperfect features—the thin straight nose, the overly full lips, the dark wide-set eyes, and the square jaw. Not to mention her tall, lanky frame. Yes, she was far from beautiful, but her hair was exquisite.

Despite the twinge of pain in her gnarled fingers, she plaited her hair expertly from years of practice. She pulled back the down comforter and climbed in between the flannel sheets. Her stomach rumbled angrily. She'd not eaten dinner again. The only time she remembered was when she ate with Jack. Thank goodness for Jack. Without him, she'd most likely starve. Ignoring hunger's grumbling, she closed her eyes and let sleep take hold.

She slipped into a world where her body no longer ached and her heart wasn't broken. She floated on a cloud, and in her dreams, she became whatever she wanted—a beautiful young girl in love. As she drifted deeper into sleep's abyss, the years melted away.

"Dance with me." Tom's eyes sparkled. The pale light cast glints of gold on his sleekly combed hair. His fine, black tuxedo, tailored to perfection, accentuated his muscular build. She'd never seen him more handsome.

He took her hand and brought it to his lips, then led her through huge double doors into a candlelit ballroom. The orchestra began to play a waltz. She placed her hand on his shoulder, and he swept her across the polished floor. Their steps matched perfectly. He pulled her closer, holding her tight, as they twirled. His warm breath tickled her ear, and she relaxed against him, content to be in his arms. They danced round and round through cotton-candy clouds, but suddenly, he was ripped from her, disappearing in a swirl of mist and fog.

"Don't go. Don't leave me," she cried.

❧☙

Alice awakened to find dawn's purple glow beaming in through her window, but her tired eyes burned as if she hadn't slept a wink. That dream! So vivid, almost as if it were real… Why, she could still feel the warmth of Tom's hand in hers, the scent of roses and beeswax candles lingering in the air, the effortless sway of their bodies moving in rhythm. She tried to drift back to the dream so that she might summon Tom again, but the moment was gone. She sighed and blinked the sleep from her eyes.

Jasper prowled onto her pillow and let out a series of loud meows. Food was a priority for the cat, if not for herself. She stepped into a pair of warm, fuzzy slippers and reached for her cane. Jasper led the way into the kitchen, where Alice poured a cup of cat food, then put the kettle on for tea. The cold, drafty room made her shiver, and she went into the parlor for a throw.

The Christmas tree sparkled in the morning light. She glanced up at the tin angel on top. Tom had given it to her before he left for war as a token of his love. Every time she looked at it, she felt as if the angel wrapped her in its golden wings, replacing her loneliness with serenity. "Forgive me," she whispered. "I know it's served no purpose to have mourned you my entire life, Tom. I should have tried to live…to love again. Not that anyone could have taken your place, but to waste my life…well, I realize now that was wrong."

The room went black. She blinked quickly, trying to make out anything: a piece of furniture, the Christmas tree, something…but it was as if she'd fallen into a cavern so deep that not even a pinpoint of light could penetrate. Had she gone blind? Perhaps she'd had a stroke. Oh Lord, was she about to die? She reached for her cane, but her hand froze on the brass handle. A piercing blue light illuminated the parlor. Oh no, it was too late. Death had claimed her.

At her feet lay the tin angel. When she reached for it, a gust of wind more powerful than a February Nor'easter blew her into an overstuffed armchair. The angel rocketed into the air and spun like a top, then burst into tiny glittering particles that fell around her in a shower of gold dust. An exquisite figure emerged—pixie-like in appearance, its gossamer wings fluttering like a butterfly's.

"What's happening?" Alice whispered, gripping the chair.

A tinkle of laughter more melodious than church bells spilled from the angel's bow-shaped lips. "Don't be frightened, Alice. I've granted your wish."

"Wish? I haven't wished for anything."

The angel floated nearer. "But you did. You wished for youth and love."

"A feeble dream."

"But a wish, nonetheless."

Alice frowned. "Maybe, but I know better than most, wishes don't come true."

The angel lifted an iridescent brow, her gaze leveled at Alice. "Really?"

With the angel's stare fixed on her, Alice glanced down over her body. Her eyes widened in disbelief. What had happened to her wrinkles and liver spots? She held out her hand. Whose smooth, supple skin was this? Next she flexed her arthritic fingers, then waggled them when no familiar stiffness stopped her. "Oh my, there's no pain," she said in disbelief.

Alice rose from the chair and, like a child filled with joy, twirled on her toes, then hurried across the room without the use of her cane and with a spring in her step that she hadn't had in years. She stopped in front of a large gilt-framed wall mirror. "It can't be true." The reflection that greeted her was one she hadn't seen in decades. Luminous smoky-gray eyes. A radiant rosy complexion accentuated by high cheekbones and a wide sensuous mouth, shiny chestnut hair… She ran her index finger over her bottom lip, down her chin and along her firm jaw.

"I don't believe it. I'm gorgeous. And young!" Tears streamed down her cheeks. This was how she'd looked in her youth, only the ugly duckling had become a swan. Times had changed and so had the standard of beauty. For the first time in her life, she liked the way she looked. But how could this be? She was ninety years old, far from young and beautiful.

Alice didn't know what to do. Part of her wanted to dash into the streets and dance: another part of her wanted to run back to bed, hide under the covers and wake up again. She looked at her agile, young hands and shook her head. She pressed her palms together and took a long look around the room. The same antique rose throw lay across the sofa. And there on the end table stood her favorite photograph of Tom in his uniform, yellowed now with age. Only she had changed.

Alice shook her head slowly, took a deep breath, and looked back at the angel. "Well, okay, maybe every once in a while miracles do happen. But why now? Why this?" She waved a smooth, wrinkle-free hand in front of herself.

"Because you've been given a second chance at life."

"A second chance? I don't understand."

"You're in limbo, Alice."

The blood drained from her face, and the room seemed to tilt. "You mean I'm dead?" Her voice came out as little more than a squeak.

Golden curls danced around the angel's face as she laughed. "Let's not call it that. Let's just say you've had a transformation."

Alice leaned against the wall to steady herself. "All right, then, this…transformation, how long will it last?"

"Till New Year's Day. Unless you find true love before then."

"What! If I haven't found love in over sixty years, how in the world can I find it in ten days?"

"It will do you no good to be negative. Besides, Tom is rooting for you."

"Tom sent you?"

The angel nodded. "A soul plagued by guilt can't rest. He wants you to love again."

"But what if I don't find love?"

The angel's radiant complexion darkened. "Then you'll forfeit this second chance—"

"And I really will be dead," Alice said glumly, finishing the tin angel's sentence. A moment later, blackness enveloped her. "Wait," she cried. "Don't leave, there's so much I need to ask you." But the darkness swallowed her useless plea. The tin angel had disappeared.

Maybe this was just another dream? She scratched the side of her leg with her fingernail. The ensuing sting confirmed she was indeed awake. She glanced at the top of the Christmas tree. The tin angel was gone. Great. She'd been given a second chance at life, but she had no idea how she was going to find love.

The piercing wail of the teakettle sent Alice sprinting to the kitchen. Steam shot from its spout, and water bubbled from its rattling lid like a science experiment gone awry. She grabbed a potholder, then lifted the copper kettle from the burner, setting it on a hot plate next to the stove.

Jasper sat on the counter, cleaning his face with his paw. If a cat could frown, that was the look he shot her between licks. Large golden eyes glared at her, and a low growl rumbled in his throat when she reached out to stroke his head.

"What's the matter, Jasp? Don't you recognize me?"

The cat inched back. "It's me," she said with a laugh, "only a new-and-improved model." She held her hand out for Jasper to sniff until he seemed satisfied she was indeed his owner.

"I've got so much I want to do. I don't know where to begin." She looked down at the fuzzy pink slippers too large for her feet and the floral nightgown barely skimming her ankles. "First off, I'd better find some clothes that fit."

She left Jasper to finish his grooming and headed toward the bedroom. Inside, she opened her closet and groaned at the stack of cardigan sweaters and stretch pants. They might be all right for an old lady, but they'd never do for a young woman about to have the time of her life. She took a moment to say a prayer of thanks for this miracle, then rummaged through a row of blouses until she came to a coral silk—the one she liked to wear when Pastor Riley came to call. He said it complemented her eyes. Yanking it off the hanger, she tossed it on the bed, then found the pair of black trousers she always wore with it.

She slipped out of her nightgown and noticed the cotton briefs about to fall down around her knees. She hadn't realized how much her waist had thickened over the years, leaving her to wonder about the changes that might have occurred to the rest of her body. She already knew her feet were smaller and she'd gained an inch or so in height. She averted her gaze to her breasts. And she knew something else—she no longer sagged.

Shopping was definitely at the top of her to-do list.

೫೦೧

Jack slid the mustard jar next to last week's leftovers, then reached for the milk. He let the refrigerator door slam shut behind him as he moved over to the kitchen table. From the corner of his eye, he saw the answering machine's flashing red light. He didn't need to play the message to know who'd left it. Bethany Snow. A long-legged blonde beauty and the daughter of Dr. Eugene Snow, dean of Chesterfield

Hall and Jack's former employer.

At one time he'd been convinced he loved Bethany, but after three years with her he'd felt more like her puppet than her fiancé. When he'd learned Silvercreek Elementary School needed a music teacher, he'd had no problem leaving Boston for the peaceful lifestyle of a small town. He was through with high-maintenance women. He'd take a simple girl any day—someone like Alice must have been. He imagined what she must have looked like in her youth, a fresh-faced beauty with an understated style. Since he'd moved in, he'd gotten pretty close to her. She needed someone to catch up on odd jobs around the old house, and he was happy to help her out. At first he'd thought of her like a grandma, but she'd become a good friend, entertaining him with stories from simpler days when life—and love—wasn't so complicated. If he could only find a woman like her, an old-fashioned girl...

He poured the milk into his coffee, then took a sip as he walked over to the answering machine. Sure enough, Bethany's smooth, silky voice filled the kitchen.

"Jack, love, I have fabulous news, and if I don't tell you now, I'll just burst. Randolph agreed to give me a few days off over the holiday. That means I can spend New Year's with you. Isn't that fabulous? It'll be like old times. Call me, love."

He took a gulp of his coffee, forgetting how hot it was. Bethany never asked for time off from her news position at WWCO Radio. Could her mission be to have him put a ring back on her finger? The thought left a queasy feeling in his stomach, similar to how he felt after eating day-old pepperoni pizza. He'd have to deal with Bethany, though, like it or not. Just not now. He was already running late. His students at school might enjoy his tardiness, but he doubted the neighboring classrooms would look favorably upon the chaos coming from his music room. Besides, he still had to drop off breakfast to

Alice.

He set his coffee cup down and grabbed the still-hot cinnamon buns he'd purchased earlier that morning from the little bakery around the corner. Renting Alice's upstairs apartment made it easy for him to check in on her and provide her with a meal. He let the door slam shut behind him and raced down the back stairs whistling "Deck the Halls."

Jack hopped up the steps to Alice's front porch and knocked on the thick wood door, listening for the tapping of her cane on the foyer floor. A few moments later, the door opened a mere six inches. An unexpected beauty with gleaming chestnut hair, full sensuous lips, and mesmerizing gray eyes peered out at him. "I-I'm here to see Alice." He felt ridiculous for his stutter, but this girl knocked the breath out of him.

"She's not here."

"Well, where is she? When will she be back?"

"I don't know. I'll tell her you came by." She snatched the cinnamon buns out of his hands, then slammed the door.

"Wait a minute. I didn't even tell you my name." He spoke to the thick mahogany door. What in the world was that all about? Something wasn't right. Alice never went anywhere. Who was that rude woman, and why was she so eager to get rid of him? And where the heck had his buns gone? She sure snatched those away quick enough. He needed some answers, and he was going to get them. Only he'd have to wait until later, as his watch showed 8:35 a.m. Just barely enough time to slip into school before the bell rang.

ℴℴ

Alice's hand shook as she set the cinnamon buns down on the kitchen table. In all the excitement, she'd forgotten about Jack. In her mind, his face flashed—dark brows rising over surprised blue eyes, mouth open about to protest—just before she'd snatched the hot rolls from his long, musician's fingers and shut him out. He would want to know what happened to Alice. To the *old* Alice… What a pickle! Jack would be back. And then what? She couldn't keep slamming the door in his face. Well, one thing was certain. She couldn't tell him the truth about her miracle transformation. But the thought of deceiving him didn't sit well with her either.

Jack was a good friend, and she didn't have many of those. She thought back to the countless times he'd come to her rescue. Like the time the pipe burst in her bathroom, and he turned off the water before the whole first floor flooded. Yes, he'd proven to be a good friend all right, but, even still, she knew he wouldn't believe her if she told him the truth. Who would? No, she had to come up with a story, and a good one at that. Thankfully, with Jack at work, she had plenty of time to think of something. Besides, she wasn't about to let this put a damper on her day. She was a young woman with lots to do!

Shaking off the doldrums, she reached for the telephone and dialed Silvercreek Cab Company. While waiting for the cab's arrival, she went into the bedroom and pulled down a shoebox from the closet shelf. She set the box on the bed and removed the lid. Inside were stacks of fifty and one-hundred-dollar bills. Alice liked to keep her money at home. She didn't trust banks, after witnessing her parent's despair at losing much of their savings in the Great Depression's run on banks.

She counted out one thousand dollars, then tucked the money into her wallet. As she returned the shoebox to the closet, she heard the honking of the cab's horn. She grabbed her purse and raced out the front door.

When she arrived at Lorelle, a high-end boutique, she selected an armful of outfits and proceeded to try each one on. With her shyness still an issue, she peeked out from the dressing room curtain to make sure the communal area with the large three-way mirror was empty before going out there to view the gorgeous evening ensemble she'd slipped into.

Alice had always avoided mirrors, yet she admired her reflection like some shallow debutante. The black ankle-length skirt she wore swirled around her legs as she moved, showing off her calves, and the matching lace blouse revealed just the right amount of skin. She'd never owned anything so beautiful—and she wouldn't now, she told herself sternly. Where in the world would she wear it? With a sigh, she turned away from the mirror and headed back toward the dressing room.

A cute young woman with a short sassy haircut and a face full of freckles rushed over to her. "Oh, miss, that outfit has your name on it. Here, let me accessorize it for you." The sales clerk took hold of her arm and led her across the store.

"I was just about to change," Alice sputtered.

"This won't take but a minute. I'm sure you'll love the result. Look." The clerk pulled a delicate gold chain from a jewelry display. She slipped it around Alice's neck, then reached for the matching earrings. "You look stunning," she cooed, holding the earrings next to Alice's face. "But you need to do something with this." She grabbed a strand of Alice's waist-length hair, tucked it inside the black lace blouse, and grinned. "Yes, that's it. I knew it." The clerk tucked in the rest of Alice's hair, then led her over to a mirror. "Now don't get me wrong. You've got beautiful hair—just too much of it. It hides your pretty face. But now, well, take a look." She stepped away so Alice could see herself.

Alice gasped. The clerk was right. She didn't need to hide behind her hair. With a shoulder-length style, it would still be long, but it wouldn't overpower her.

"You like?"

Speechless, Alice could only nod.

The clerk pulled a business card from her pocket and placed it in Alice's palm. "This is Frederick. He's a fabulous hairdresser. Tell him Kendra sent you. He'll take extra-good care of you. Now, will you be putting today's purchases on your credit card?"

"No, cash." Alice entered the dressing room with her head awhirl. She had less than two weeks to find true love, and she was about to buy an outfit she didn't need and cut twelve inches off her hair. Had she gone mad? Or maybe she was doing exactly what she needed to do in order to attract the man of her dreams.

ഇരുCS

At the salon, true to Kendra's word, Alice was given the royal treatment, beginning with a lengthy shampoo and fabulous scalp massage. She listened to the steady *snip, snip, snip* of Frederick's shears as he cut her hair. Her eyes were squeezed shut and her heart was pounding, yet it wasn't fear she felt but excitement. As each section of hair dropped to the floor, a weight lifted. Old insecurities disappeared, and, like a butterfly emerging from its cocoon, she too was free.

With the final click of the shears, she snuck a glance.

"No, no," Frederick shrieked, spinning her chair away from the mirror. He stood with hands on hips, tapping the toe of his heavily studded cowboy boot. "You mustn't peek till I'm ready for the reveal." He spoke with a heavy European accent that she thought he used more for effect than from living abroad.

"Sorry," she murmured, sinking into the chair. The sleeve of his polyester shirt—the likes of which she hadn't seen for decades—brushed her cheek as he worked mousse through her hair.

He grabbed the blow dryer as if he were drawing a pistol and held it beside his leather-clad thigh. "Now, tip your head down to your knees, and let me finish this masterpiece."

Alice bent down and studied the veins in the marble floor while

Frederick worked his magic on her hair.

"Here we go, Miss Alice. Sit up and toss your head back." When she obliged, he turned her toward the mirror. "Voila."

His smile reminded her of the Cheshire cat's, and she definitely felt like Alice in Wonderland, but her hairstyle was a work of art.

Mountains of glossy chestnut hair skimmed her shoulders. Not too short. Not too long. Perfect. Just perfect. "I don't know what to say."

"Ahh, no need for words. Your eyes say it all, and with the right shadow, they could seduce a man with a glance." Frederick snapped his fingers. A pretty young girl with flawless skin came running. "Take Miss Alice to the makeup counter and make her siz-z-le."

By the time Alice left the salon, she barely recognized herself—glossed lips, sultry eyes and cheekbones a cover model would die for. Too bad she didn't have anyone to show off her new look to.

At home, she dropped her armful of packages on the sofa. Jasper jumped off the windowsill and strolled around her feet. He didn't rub against her legs as usual but kept his distance, as if trying to make out this latest change in her appearance.

"It's all right. It's me. Get used to it, my friend, this new look is here to stay. At least for ten days or so," she said glumly. A chilly bolt lanced through her. The reality of her limited time dimmed the glow of the tin angel's miracle. If she didn't find true love by New Year's...

To rid herself of her melancholy, Alice waltzed over to her old record player and put on Frank Sinatra. As she swayed to the music, she opened her packages. She pulled out outfit after outfit, holding each one up, then tossing it toward the sofa. Some made it to the cushions, but many landed on the floor.

Alice undid the buttons on her coral blouse, then unzipped her trousers. "Away with the old," she sang, slipping out of her clothes and tossing them into the air, "and in with the new." She picked up an animal-print shirt, held it up to her chest, then twirled around the parlor in her underwear.

A knock on the front door froze her. Every muscle tensed. For a moment, she was taken back to the night her world shattered—the night Tom had been taken from her. She'd been about the same age, but this was a new day, and it wouldn't be a solemn-faced sergeant bringing bad news. Oh Lord, it must be Jack. She dropped the shirt and raced to the bedroom for her robe. She wasn't prepared for a visitor. And she still didn't know what she was going to tell him.

…Excerpt from *TIN ANGEL* by Raine English.

Available in ebook and print.

ABOUT THE AUTHOR

Award-winning author Raine English always wanted to be a writer. She began her career as a journalist, but writing romance novels was her passion. Her stories have won many awards, including finalling in the Romance Writers of America® Golden Heart® and winning the Daphne du Maurier Award.

She enjoys writing both adult and young adult contemporary romance infused with elements of magic and the paranormal, along with eerie Gothic historical novels.

When not behind her computer, you can find her reading, usually something involving the supernatural. She lives in New England with her family, two dogs, and a mischievous cat.

Raine would love to hear from you! She can be reached at Raine@RaineEnglish.com.

Visit Raine's website at www.RaineEnglish.com
Follow Raine on Twitter at https://twitter.com/RaineEnglish
Join Raine on Facebook at www.facebook.com/RaineEnglish